April blinked at him and tried to discern what he'd asked.

"You don't have anywhere pressing to be, do you?"

She opened and closed her mouth like a fish gasping for water, but shook her head. If only Malachi knew just how not pressing her time was. She was sure her driver was long gone, and even if he wasn't, she didn't have anywhere to go. And it would be days before she could schedule another driver if Malachi insisted she couldn't rent the store.

"*Jah*, I am okay with helping Esther watch the *boppli*. Are you?" she asked, taking care of how she phrased her words to allow the older woman her dignity when it was so obvious she yearned for it. "After all, you said you didn't trust me. Suppose I might steal away with all your wealth."

Malachi burst into laughter. "And I guess if you can find anything worth taking except little Jeb and Aunt Esther, you can have it. But let's be clear on one thing—I never said I didn't trust you, I said I didn't know you."

Christina Rich lives in northeast Kansas. Her passion for stories comes from a rich past of reading and digging through odd historical tidbits, where she finds a treasure trove of inspiration. She loves photography, art, ancestry research and, of course, writing happy-ever-afters.

Books by Christina Rich

Love Inspired

A Husband for an Amish Bride
His Amish Marriage Offer

Love Inspired Historical

The Guardian's Promise
The Warrior's Vow
Captive on the High Seas
The Negotiated Marriage
The Marshal's Unexpected Bride
A Family for the Twins

Visit the Author Profile page at LoveInspired.com.

HIS AMISH MARRIAGE OFFER

CHRISTINA RICH

Recycling programs for this product may not exist in your area.

ISBN-13: 978-1-335-62144-3

His Amish Marriage Offer

For questions and comments about the quality of this book, please contact us at CustomerService@Harlequin.com.

Love Inspired
22 Adelaide St. West, 41st Floor
Toronto, Ontario M5H 4E3, Canada
www.LoveInspired.com

HarperCollins Publishers
Macken House, 39/40 Mayor Street Upper,
Dublin 1, D01 C9W8, Ireland
www.HarperCollins.com

Printed in Lithuania

For I was an hungred, and ye gave me meat:
I was thirsty, and ye gave me drink:
I was a stranger, and ye took me in:
Naked, and ye clothed me: I was sick, and ye
visited me: I was in prison, and ye came unto me.

—*Matthew* 25:35–36

To my wonderful critique partners who are writing their own exciting adventures. Marie Wells Couto, Kimberly Keagan and Denise Colby, thank you for everything! The brainstorming, the suggestions and never-ending support!

Carolyn Bolen, thank you for sharing your reminiscences and inspiring ideas, like cutting roses.

Chapter One

"You need a wife!"

Malachi Stoltzfus glanced up from his color-coded calendar and smiled at his great aunt. Ever since little Jeb had arrived on his doorstep three months before, Aunt Esther had hounded him about getting married. She'd even gone so far as to bring him a list of the eligible, non-courting Amish ladies from Anderson County. The fact that she'd taken her search outside of their church community told him how desperate she was to marry him off. He flashed a smile before pecking her on the cheek. "*Gut* morning, Aunt Esther. How are you this fine day?"

"Peachy. Absolutely peachy. I'd be a lot better if we settled you into a fine marriage. Married, you know. You need a wife, and that little boy needs a *mamm*."

Malachi penciled in a note on next Tuesday's orange block. His calendar was filling up quickly, leaving him little time for his nephew. He gazed down into Jeb's wide brown eyes. His heart swelled with a fatherly pride that should belong to Jared, his wastrel brother. But Malachi would not complain. He loved Jeb and there were days he wondered how he'd ever gone on in life without the little guy. He couldn't recall the days before him. But he also couldn't help the fear that one day Jared or the *boppli's mamm* would show up and reclaim him, or that Bishop Mueller would decree Malachi an unfit parent. He pushed the fear aside and smiled. "We're doing just fine, aren't we, little one? Besides, I don't have time to look around."

"That's why I've done it for you," she said. "Did you look over the list?"

He had, but he would not give her the satisfaction of knowing it. "I don't have time to court."

And that was the truth. Nearing thirty-three years old, he didn't have the need or patience to court a woman. He wasn't a peacock out to preen his feathers to attract a *fraa.* It just wasn't in him.

Aunt Esther snorted. "And what are you going to do with him next week, now that your schedule is full?"

"Do what I've done for the last few months. Find a babysitter."

"That will never do. School is about to start. Besides, my great great-nephew needs a mother, not a part-time watcher. He needs coddling and someone to sing to him."

Malachi lifted his free hand into the air in mock surrender and smiled at Jeb. "We sing, don't we, Jeb?"

Jeb fussed, and Malachi propped him against his shoulder. "There now. Aunt Esther is only joking. Aren't you?"

She ignored his pointed look, then pursed one side of her mouth. "I suppose I may be, but I found you a more permanent solution."

His breakfast turned in his stomach. What had she done this time? He didn't mind the help, but he didn't like Aunt Esther's interference either. A list of potential *fraas* was one thing, but he feared what she was up to now. "I can manage, Aunt Esther."

Shaking her head, she tsked. "If only I were thirty years younger, I'd be of some more help, and I wouldn't push the issue. I promised your *mamm* I would look out for her boys. I failed one," she said, laying her gnarled hand on Jeb's back.

A cringe rocked Malachi's core. Jared hadn't been Aunt Esther's responsibility. He'd been Malachi's. Malachi was the one who'd failed.

"Who knows where Jeb's *daed* is or if he is coming back." She paused. Her blue as midnight gaze, faded with age, touched his and held them. "I will not fail you, Malachi Stoltzfus. I will not fail any more *kinder* of my heart. You hear me? You've grown in age, and it is past time you marry."

"But I don't want a wife." A wife would be one more opportunity to fail in his responsibilities. Marriage would force him back into the spotlight of their community, even if only until the courtship and wedding were over. It was more time than he wished to be under the *gmay*'s sometimes crude magnifying glass. He'd already spent too much time there, being pitied and gawked at when his *daed* had refused to seek forgiveness from the community and left the church for the *Englischer*'s ways.

He'd been pitied and gawked at even more when his *mamm* battled depression until her mental faculties declined enough to keep her from getting out of bed, leaving him to care for Jared. Malachi had heard the whispers behind cupped hands, saying *Mamm* died of a broken heart, but he didn't think so, and he never corrected the bishop out of fear of more unwanted attention. *Mamm* had said she never could hold her head up again and face her shame. Malachi knew his *mamm* had died of embarrassment, and he was fairly certain there'd been more to her death than anyone knew. The handwritten note, still tucked in the back of his Bible, that she'd left behind told him all he needed to know. Suicide wasn't common among their people, but neither was the type of abuse or neglect she'd suffered at his father's hands.

"That is beside the fact. You need a wife."

Adjusting Jeb into the crook of his elbow, Malachi massaged his neck, then pointed to his calendar. "Business is *gut*, *jah*?"

His construction business was flourishing, and for a time, the past was not muddying the Stoltzfus name. People waved and smiled at him when he passed by. They recommended him, and he'd had to do the one thing he'd never thought would happen: purchase an *Englischer* phone to keep up with his calls. The bishop was more than understanding and even had suggested it. But Aunt Esther was right. If he was going to keep up with the work, he needed to find someone to care for Jeb. "I can afford a nanny."

But that was a problem, too. It was difficult to trust just anyone with Jeb, even the young women he'd grown up with. Especially with the Stoltzfus reputation. He didn't want Jeb to hear anything bad about his family. Not about his *grossdaddi*, his *daed*, or even Malachi. What would negative words do to the infant? Leave him feeling as if he were an outcast for sins not his own?

Just like Malachi often felt.

The air left his lungs. If he weren't holding his nephew, he would have hit his knees and cried. The burden on his shoulders was too much, even at thirty-two, and he wasn't sure how he could keep walking tall, especially with the shame he carried on behalf of his parents and his brother. One thing was for certain—He understood *Mamm* a little more. She just hadn't been strong enough. Or he and Jared hadn't been enough to draw her from her depression.

He looked in wonder at the innocent little boy cradled in the crook of his arm. He, too, endured his father's and grandfather's sins. At least he would when he became older. Jeb was nothing more than a reminder to the community of the irresponsible and unreliable nature of the Stoltzfus men. Malachi had spent most of his childhood and all his adulthood trying to rectify the church's perception of him by being a good, responsible Amish man and being a good brother to Jared, but it had done little for him.

Aunt Esther nodded. "I thought you may see things my way."

Malachi frowned his thoughts away. "You know of a nanny?"

Maybe someone who knew nothing about their family? At that moment, a young woman pressed her face to the dirty glass of his storefront window. She cupped her hands around her eyes as if to ward off the glaring sun. She didn't smile but looked as if she'd eaten a sour piece of candy. "Excuse me, Aunt Esther, she looks lost."

"Bah, no one gets lost in Garnett, especially on the outskirts of town." Aunt Esther waved him off and opened the door for the woman. A large black suitcase wrapped several times over with frayed twine weighed down her arm. She was petite, yet curvy. Copper curls sprang from her dark *kapp.* Green eyes glittered under dark eyelashes. She looked oddly familiar, but he didn't recall seeing her around Garnett, Kansas. Maybe she was visiting family.

"Hello," he said. "Are you lost?"

The woman looked at him, then Aunt Esther. "Are you Esther Beiler? David Beiler's aunt? The one with the store I can rent for my business?"

His brow scrunched downward. "Huh?"

Aunt Esther cackled as she wrapped an arm around the young woman's shoulders. "Malachi, meet April Beiler."

His cousin David's widow? What was she doing here?

It'd been a few years since the wedding, and he'd only met her the one time. He'd offered quick congratulations to them before moving on to talk business with other cousins and uncles at the wedding.

"It's about time you arrived, April." Aunt Esther released April and stepped back with her arms crossed, looking the young woman up and down. "I was beginning to worry."

"I'm sorry," April said, her voice soft and timid. She

set the suitcase on the refinished hardwood floor, then fidgeted with it to keep it in place before resting her hand on her swollen belly. "My driver's car broke down on the side of the road. I had to walk a bit."

Malachi wasn't unsympathetic to her plight and should offer her a glass of sun-soaked tea, but he had a feeling he couldn't afford to be distracted. He narrowed his eyes. "Aunt Esther, what are you up to?"

"Nothing more than what needs doing. You need a wif—nanny, and I've offered April the use of my shop." His aunt motioned toward the adjoining building connected by a pair of old French doors he'd refinished a few years ago. "Once you get it cleared out, mind you. In exchange for keeping Jeb and watching that noisemaker of yours while you do actual work."

"Noisemaker" was his aunt's term for the *Englischer* phone, but he wasn't about to correct her since his breakfast was rolling around in his stomach like an off-balanced buggy wheel. He thought he actually might be ill. There had been times over the last few months he'd wondered if Aunt Esther's memory was slipping. He didn't like this idea. It only solidified her age and frailty, and he wasn't ready to accept the fact that the woman who'd helped raise him and his brother was losing her strength of mind when she'd always been sharp as a tack and had allowed nothing to pass her notice. "You mean my shop? Or did you forget again?"

The pair of attached buildings had been a single home built by his grandfather and later divided into two spaces, then given to his *mamm* after his grandfather's death. They'd lived upstairs as a family until his father had left. After his *mamm* died, he and his brother had moved to the house across the alley where Aunt Esther lived. Malachi barely stepped foot into the other half of the building where his *mamm* had made her quilts and displayed them for purchase. He'd battled with himself when Aunt Esther used it for her sewing business after *mamm*'s death. Now, it stored his *mamm*'s and Jared's belongings, and he wasn't ready to deal with the boxes.

"Y-yo-your shop?" April stammered, moistening her lips as her gaze bounced between him and Aunt Esther. He really should offer her a glass of tea. "You mean it isn't yours?"

Oh, boy. April's eyes, as big as Aunt Esther's giant chocolate-chip cookies, filled to the brim. If she blinked, the tears would roll down her cheeks. He'd had enough of crying women to last him a lifetime. He never knew how to console them. Couldn't, which had been clear by his failed attempts to get his *mamm* to quit crying night after night when he'd been a boy.

April paled as she looked at the doors dividing the two spaces.

Aunt Esther clamped her lips together in a tight line as if to tell him he'd gone and stuck his foot in his mouth with his all-too-blunt way of speaking. He felt like he was a boy of eight caught sneaking frogs into the house again. Even worse, the twist of his aunt's lips and the squint of her eye to a specific degree told him she had the final word and there was nothing more to say.

She hadn't forgotten the adjoining shop next door was his. She'd only used it for a time when she'd taken on mending clothes and making quilts before her health had become a factor. He dropped his glance down the length of April, noting her mourning dress and her overly swollen belly. David and their two-year-old little girl had died in a horrific fire several months back. He'd heard that from Esther. He hadn't heard, though, that David and April were expecting. Although he hadn't seen his cousin since the wedding, Malachi had mourned him and done his duty to help financially support his cousin's *fraa*. He hadn't forgotten about the assistance; he set aside from every job *Gotte* blessed him with. But getting on with his life, he had forgotten the why and where of the financial support, only making note to give Aunt Esther the envelope upon completion of his work.

"It just so happens, she's a widow in need of a husband before the *boppli* comes." Aunt Esther's papery-wrinkled cheeks bunched into a ball. Hidden beneath the crevices was a smile. A too-pleased smile. "And for your information, a wife is cheaper than a nanny, you know."

April's cheeks turned crimson red. "I—I'm not here for a husband."

"Oh, posh! Every woman needs a husband, especially one in your condition."

Malachi bounced Jeb in his arms when he fussed. He stared at April's hand and the large, swollen belly it rested on. "I didn't know his widow was pregnant."

"I am," April said, shifting her weight from one foot to the other.

Aunt Esther shook her head. "It is only by *Gotte*'s grace and Milda's letter that I even discovered April's state. Now, how about I bake two pies at once? You need a wife, and she needs a husband."

At least his aunt knew a pregnant widow was descending on her doorstep. She'd been mentally prepared. Malachi wasn't.

"I do not need a wife, Aunt Esther. We're getting along just fine on our own," he said, propping Jeb against his shoulder. He caught sight of April's tattered suitcase and scowled. "And just where did you think to house Cousin April if your little plan worked?" He hoped reminding Aunt Esther April was kin would stop her matchmaking scheme. "It's not like you have a lot of room in your house."

His aunt would, if her extra rooms weren't full of her crafting supplies. One room was set aside for canning, while another held mending customers had forgotten to fetch. The other room had been off limits, to him and Jared even as children. They'd never asked what was behind the locked door.

"Well, I had hoped—" she waggled her eyebrows, then winked "—you would do right by your duty as her kinsman and marry her. Then there'd be no question where she would stay."

Malachi mentally smacked his palm against his forehead and snorted. "Kinsman, like the kinsman redeemer? Like Boaz and Ruth?"

A gasp cut through the air, and when Malachi realized it wasn't his, he looked at April. She appeared as shocked as he felt. *Gut*, they were of one mind, at least in this matter. Neither one of them wanted to get married.

* * *

April's mind spun with the semblance of cows trampling through the field. She'd come here with the promise of owning her own shop and handling her finances, and if she guessed correctly, her possible future stood on the other side of the beautifully crafted double doors.

The ability to make choices without being rammed into a wall anytime she wanted to cook something different was being manipulated from her by a matchmaking aunt. April hadn't come here for the promise of another husband who would dictate her every movement and word. She did not know Aunt Esther had meant to marry her off, and to David's cousin, no less. She shifted toward the door, wondering if she could make the two miles outside of town before her driver's car was fixed and headed back to Haven, Kansas.

April certainly hadn't expected this turn of events. The lure of having a shop space to make her own had banished all practicality on her part. She'd left an almost perfectly good bed at Milda's house—a bed she would have abandoned upon the *boppli*'s arrival, but a bed and a roof over her head nonetheless—and she'd abandoned it for uncertainty. An uncertainty she hadn't expected, but now she did not know what she was going to do. A lump lodged in her throat, and she tried to swallow it.

"Are you telling me there isn't a shop for me to rent?" April asked.

"Yes," he said.

"No," Aunt Esther said over the brooding man's dark tone. "It's perfectly fine for you to use the space. I'm not using it." She pointed a finger at Malachi. "He isn't using it—at least, not for any good purpose."

April rubbed her temple. It had been more than an hour since she'd left her driver and begun the walk to Garnett while he waited for help with his car. Surely, help had come, and her driver would be heading back to Haven. If she found a phone and called him, would he come back for her and take her home?

Home? What home?

What did she have to go back to? Milda's broom closet, and the resentment her adopted community seemed to brew at needing to care for her.

No.

Milda's room had been spoken for the moment Esther had invited April to Garnett. No one else in the community had room for a widow with a *boppli* on the way, and even if they did, they didn't want to make room for her. Besides, the entire ride here, she'd been hopeful for a new start.

Hopeful, because she had no choice but to move forward.

She couldn't look back.

She couldn't keep on the path she'd been on, aimlessly residing at Milda's while waiting for her future to come her way. *Gotte* found it in His will to place a flashing stop sign on her road when David and their little girl died. That sign had made her stop and reflect on the choices she'd made, ones that hadn't been the best. It made her realize she needed to be more intentional about her decisions rather than make emotional knee-jerk ones because she felt unwanted.

Now it was just her and the *boppli* in a new place, far from bad memories. Well, she didn't need her former community's pity any more than she needed Malachi's *brooding*. She didn't need anyone. Especially a husband. Not if Esther was still willing to lend her the use of her storefront for business. Well, not Esther's store, but Malachi's. She gave him a once-over before settling her attention on his stormy blue eyes—eyes almost the color of steel wool, but blue enough to not be gray. She inhaled as much as the *boppli* in her belly allowed her to and tried to settle her anxiousness.

"I—I have a suggestion." The borrowed suitcase rocked against her leg and nearly fell over when she shifted her weight. The old thing held the last of her possessions, all salvaged from the fire. She reached down to support it. A missing metal foot had made it awkward to stand as it should, but she didn't mind. She didn't even mind the twine keeping the sides closed tightly together. She was grateful for the use of it.

Assured the bag wouldn't fall over, she stretched her aching fingers and clenched them again. The burns snaking around her wrist and up her arm were still red and raw whenever she overtaxed them. Today's warm weather, the walk, her pregnancy and the unknown taxed the healing flesh and made her wish for a quiet dark place to rest and massage the salve she'd made until she could ignore the searing pain that occasionally plagued her. She drew in another hesitant breath and focused on Esther. The woman seemed the more reasonable of the two.

"It's obvious your nephew doesn't want a wife," she

said as she closed her eyes against the terrifying emotions that often attacked her whenever the mention of her marrying again made its way into conversation. She bit the inside of her cheek and willed the rising anxiety in her chest to release her from its horrible grip. "And it is too soon for me to marry. I will watch the baby for the use of the shop. I'm sure we'll get along nicely. Of course, I will find my own sleeping arrangements." She hoped the shop area was decent and able to house her for a time until she could find a room to rent.

Malachi's eyes darkened as he eyed her. Caution, suspicion, and maybe even anger, pressed crow's feet to the corners of his eyes. His tanned face told her he spent a lot of time out in the sun. He glanced at her wide stomach, and his cheek twitched.

"How can you manage Jeb in your condition?"

Esther hooted until she lost her breath. "Son, you should be ashamed of yourself for asking a woman that sort of question. Women have managed households just fine without the aid of men. I thought I taught you better."

He flinched, then quickly schooled his face back to the stonelike structure he'd maintained since her arrival. Was he always so stiff and unyielding? April tucked her hands into the folds of her black skirts. She prayed he hadn't noticed her burns and wouldn't suggest they would keep her from doing her job. "I assure you it's not the first time a woman has cared for one *boppli*, while carrying another, and keeping shop and household chores. I am more than capable, *Cousin* Malachi. My *mamm* had two sets of twins under the age of six and saw fit to keep her home and the family business going while my *daed* busied himself with the farm."

Her childhood home still overflowed with *kinder*. She had four *bruders* and *schwesters* young enough to remain at home with her *daed* and Millie, his new *fraa*, and her own five children. Although her parents had asked her to return home within days after the fire, she'd already determined that wasn't an option. Besides, there was no room, and with the drought hitting *Daed*'s crops hard, there was little extra to eat, and she refused to be a burden to anyone. Ever again. She hadn't liked how David had made her feel during their marriage, always in the way, always at fault for one thing or another. She didn't ever want to feel that way again. She would do things on her own. She had to.

Scratching the back of his neck, Malachi shook his head. "I wouldn't feel right, April. I won't take advantage of you." His gaze fell to her stomach, and April wondered if her pregnancy scared him. "Or your condition."

"My *condition* is completely natural, I assure you." She rubbed her belly for effect, then stepped forward to gauge his reaction. He wasted no time placing the beautiful rustic counter between them. The smile teasing the corners of her mouth gave way to an unexpected giggle. *That was fun!* And it was. For the first time in a long time, since before David had arrived at her *daed*'s farm asking to marry her without courting, she sensed a small bit of freedom. The freedom to tease and laugh. Joy tickled her conscience. But she quickly sobered when she recalled she didn't have the right to such freedoms. David was gone. So was their first child. This was David's family, and she didn't want them to think she didn't mourn him. She lifted an eyebrow. "I assure you, I am not contagious."

Esther threw back her head and bellowed. Once she gained her breath and composure, she smacked her hand on the counter and pierced her nephew with a sparkling stare. "She has spunk, Malachi."

"She has something," Malachi grumbled beneath his breath. "But my answer is no. I'll ask Bishop Mueller about a nanny, and about a place for you to stay until arrangements can be made for you to go back home."

The idea of having her own store slipped away. Would he really make her return to Haven, Kansas? To Milda's house? Milda would find her another room, but as much as she appreciated the older lady's generosity, April didn't know how much longer she could stay in the small room, especially with the *boppli* coming soon. "You wouldn't be taking advantage of me, not when we're bartering one service for another. You would be doing me a favor by allowing me to start my business."

His jaw molded into a familiar stubborn set, and without thinking, she took a step back. She'd seen it a thousand times when David's dogged resolve grabbed hold of an idea and he was determined to make her see his way of thinking, too. Like the time when, against all caution, he'd sold several of their horses and nearly everything in their home, including her mother's quilts, to buy a herd of goats. Even now, her heart ached a little at losing the quilts she'd brought into their marriage. She hadn't minded sacrificing for their household if needed, but David hadn't known the first thing about goats and the ones he'd purchased hadn't produced milk like he'd said they would. Instead, they'd eaten everything, even the neighbor's vegetable garden. For which David blamed her, as if she'd been the one with the idea or known how to contain them on their farm.

Malachi's chest expanded in a deep breath, drawing her attention to the wide breadth pulling his vest tight. He was broad and tall, and an overall giant of a man. His dark brown hair curled, resting on his collar. David had been nowhere near the height of this man, and he hadn't resembled his cousin much either. She moistened her lips and wondered if Malachi held other differences from David. Were they alike in character? Although she could tell the situation frustrated him, she didn't see any signs of railing or bruising fists. Could she reason with Malachi and make him see the benefits of having her rent his empty storefront?

"My answer is—" An *Englischer*'s phone jingled, cutting off his words.

April glanced around the shop area before returning her focus to Malachi. He pulled his mouth into a tight line and fished a little black rectangle from beneath the counter and tapped the screen. "This is Malachi."

Even though she knew some Amish could use phones for business, she couldn't hide her surprise. She studied Malachi as he listened to the phone. His brow rippled like water pushed by the wind. Worry lines creased the corners of his eyes. He glanced down at the baby in his arm and the tension softened with his smile. It was obvious he loved the child a great deal.

She thought about David and their little girl, Samantha. His excitement about their first *boppli* had flattened like a pancake the moment he'd realized they'd had a daughter. Other than at dinner, he rarely spent time with her. Not that April blamed him. It was his way, being the only child of elderly parents. But Sam…she'd been April's ray of sunshine glinting off the tall grasses in the golden hour just before the sun slipped beyond the horizon. That time of the evening was extraordinary and captivating, just like Sam had been. It was as if the entire world paused while the sun gently caressed the Earth one last time before she said good-night.

"April." Malachi's deep timbre jolted her from her thoughts. He looked unsure, hesitant, as he glanced above Esther's shoulder then back to April. "It seems there is an emergency at the Miller's—one of my job sites—and the guys are on another job. I'm afraid Jeb is too heavy for Esther to hold."

"Bah, you just don't want me strolling around town with the little guy. Afraid I may leave him somewhere."

The high color rising in his cheeks said Esther was right. He cleared his throat. "April, do you…do you mind watching Jeb an hour or two until I can get things squared away?"

"*Jah*," April said, and before he could second-guess himself and take this opportunity from her, she continued with, "I can do it."

His mouth twisted. "I realize we don't know each other, but Aunt Esther is right, I can't leave my nephew with her."

"Nephew?" she whispered. Her wondering renewed over the way he adored the child.

"Yes, my nephew." He glanced at the older woman. "What say you, Aunt Esther?"

Esther cleared her throat. "I'm not nearly as strong as I used to be, Malachi, and I get forgetful at times when my mind wanders. But I can help April."

He scrubbed his free hand over his face. "Well, I guess there is nothing else to be done, *jah*?"

Esther hooted in that odd cackle and held her arms out for the *boppli*. "I knew you'd see things my way."

"Now, Aunt Esther." Malachi's tone deepened to a warning level. Gooseflesh danced along April's arms as she paid close attention to the interaction between Malachi and his aunt, but the old lady smiled, her eyes twinkling.

"I know, I know. You don't need a wife, and this old lady needs to quit interfering."

"*Jah*, you would save me the pain of headaches," he teased. "But you need to sit down before I hand Jeb to you." Malachi waited for Aunt Esther to sit on a cushioned, spindle-backed rocker before slipping Jeb into his aunt's arms. April marveled at the tender way Malachi pressed his mouth to his aunt's papery brow before he straightened. *"Denki."*

David would have stalked away, his boot heels hammering against the floor, so everyone in the county knew something displeased him.

"Are you all right with this?"

April blinked at him and tried to discern what he'd asked.

"You don't have anywhere pressing to be, do you?"

She opened and closed her mouth, like a fish gasping for water, but shook her head. If only Malachi knew just how not pressing her time or place was. She was sure her driver was long gone, and even if he weren't, she didn't have anywhere to go. And it would be days before she could schedule another driver if Malachi insisted she couldn't rent the store.

"*Jah*, I am okay with helping Esther watch the *boppli*. Are you?" she asked, taking care of how she phrased her words to allow the older woman her dignity when it was so obvious she yearned for it. "After all, you said you didn't trust me. Suppose I may steal away with all your wealth."

Malachi burst into laughter. "And I guess if you can find anything worth taking except little Jeb and Aunt Esther...well, you can have it. But let's be clear on one thing, I never said I didn't trust you, I said I didn't know you."

And before she could consider the differences, and voice how in her mind, there were none, Malachi bent, kissed the infant's head, and said his goodbyes with a, "See ya in a while." She watched him don his straw hat and slip out the door, his heels silent as his walk was easy and light, and she wondered if he included the storefront next door worthy of anything, too.

Chapter Two

"If I had known the store didn't belong to you, I wouldn't have come all this way," April said as she perched on the edge of a long, pale-colored bench sitting beneath the wide window. She glanced around the square footage and wondered what other choice she'd had but to come here.

Even though Esther was David's aunt and not her own, the *boppli* April carried was the older woman's relative, and she'd offered April an opportunity she couldn't refuse. If only she had considered the offer wasn't real, she would have saved herself a lot of disappointment. But her time in Haven had taxed her, especially when good-intentioned people reminded her of all she'd lost. It'd been *Gotte*'s will. Haven's Bishop Yoder had reminded her often enough. That was their belief. And she believed that, but how could she respond to the constant looks of pity whenever someone approached her, other than to nod and smile? They hadn't known the true source of her grief or her guilt. They hadn't known the turmoil of living with David. They hadn't known the guilt she'd felt at being free of the man she'd grown to love because she was free of his constant criticism and displeasure.

Samantha was another matter.

Her little girl. Her sweet, sweet little girl.

Oh, how her heart ached to hold her one more time, to kiss her brow and smooth her downy-soft hair back from her chubby little cheeks. As much as she might regret marrying David Beiler—a man who'd been looking for a wife, according to a friend of a friend—she never could regret she'd borne their child.

"Oh, the store is mine," Esther said, snapping April from her musing.

Esther's mouth thinned and her brow furrowed, as if she were trying to remember a distant memory. When she tilted her head and raised an eyebrow, April nearly asked her if she was all right, but then Esther nodded as if she'd been holding a conversation with herself. April had seen Milda do this a few times and wondered if it was common among the elders.

"My treadle sewing machine is over there." She motioned toward the dark-stained double doors with more windows than the home April had shared with David. She liked lots of windows and bright, natural sunlight. It shooed away the dank darkness and the shadows. "Bolts of fabrics and customer's mending. Business had been good that last year before the boys started working. It could be again, if a young woman like yourself took over the tasks of mending."

April wanted to say she didn't intend to open a sewing shop, but feared her intention might sway Esther to Malachi's way of thinking. Esther stared at her trembling hand poking out from beneath the baby's tiny shoulder. How did she manage threading a needle with her gnarled and disfigured hands? April's own hand twitched, and she gripped her skirts to bury her scars. And the shame of placing judgment on Esther. How many times had she encountered people who thought she couldn't do things because of her badly scarred hands?

Esther bent her head. The strings of her *kapp* dangled toward the baby's face as she cooed at Jeb. "Malachi isn't using it, and he won't mind having you take it over. Of that, I'm certain. It'll be *gut* for his business, too. He builds homes and does renovations, and you'll provide things for the homes. It's a win-win. In my way of thinking."

Unable to track Esther's conversation, April furrowed her brow. Malachi claimed the store was his, but Esther said it was hers. Had April somehow become entangled in a family disagreement? She certainly hoped not.

"That is some relief, I suppose." April wasn't too certain about Esther's way of thinking, though. What Malachi did and what Esther wanted to do were as far from the other as Haven was from Garnett. Maybe even farther. It was like buying a goat and expecting eggs, but she wouldn't say as much, because she knew that wasn't quite right either. Maybe Esther had a good idea, and she and Malachi could bring in customers for each other.

April leaned over the arm of the bench and slid her suitcase underneath it. "Although that still leaves me without a bed to sleep in." Homeless. It wasn't the first time in the last months she'd sensed her compass had broken into tiny fragments. The ravaging fire had taken her home and immediate family. All she had left were the items in her borrowed suitcase and the *boppli* residing in her womb.

"Nonsense." Esther waved a free hand. "If you're not too tired, I'll show you the shop area. Then we will go to my house for some lunch and discuss the arrangements. If this little guy allows us time, we'll have one of my spare rooms cleaned up in no time."

Exhaustion ate at April and cramped her muscles, but a niggling of hope stirred again. Her own store. Her own source of income. Freedom. She was so close to taking a step in the right direction, but a tall, dark-haired man stood between her and her hopes. However, curiosity at what her own little shop might look like loomed over the image of Malachi and his refusal to let her rent it. She couldn't say no to Esther. Besides, the lure of lunch fueled her, restoring hope by leaps.

"That sounds *wunderbar*." The *boppli* stretched and kicked inside her belly. "Of course, I may need moments to rest, but we'll accomplish what we set out to do." April stood from the bench and lifted Jeb out of Esther's arms. Her heart sighed in contentment as he snuggled into her. Motherhood was such a precious gift, and so fragile. She wondered where Jeb's parents were, and why Malachi cared for him now.

"Does Malachi use this side?" she asked, glancing around what appeared to be an office. A well-crafted table sat toward the back wall with a custom chair pushed against the edge. She smiled at the unpretentious limestone rock weighing down the neatly stacked pile of papers. A counter, with a simple, color-coded calendar, hung on the wall, portioning off what looked to be a kitchen area, and she wondered if this had been a home at one time. All the dark wooden doors with old, round, brass knobs led her to believe it had been a house once, but what impressed her most was the organization and cleanliness of it all. Malachi Stoltzfus might be stubborn, as proven by their conversation, but his place of business was spotless and put together.

"Yes," Esther said, shaking her head. "We can leave your suitcase here. I'll have Malachi bring it over later, unless you need something before then. I imagine Jeb and your baggage are more than you should carry at the moment."

"*Denki*," April said as Esther opened a door and pulled out a stroller from inside. She motioned for her to fasten the baby in. Then, pushing the stroller with Jeb inside it, April followed Esther through the double doors.

April's eyes widened the moment she crossed the threshold. The space was vast, with high ceilings and had a circular area with windows nearly stretching from the floor to ceiling that would make a perfect location for a bassinet for her *boppli*. The little space looked out onto a terrace overgrown with random flowers and greenery, and she imagined placing a rocker facing the window so she could greet the birds and butterflies as they visited the garden. She wondered if Malachi would mind her placing a hummingbird feeder and maybe planting some flowers in the boxes to attract butterflies. She turned around and noticed a small counter with an old register in the middle of the floor. Floor-to-ceiling shelves formed two walls, enough space to display inventory. She drew in a deep breath. "It's beautiful."

"It is. Malachi's *grossdaddi* was a *gut* carpenter and made all the wooden items you see. Malachi did some restoration. Mostly in the other half, though. He gets his natural craftsmanship from his *grossdaddi*."

April could barely tell the difference between the old and the new wood, evidence of Malachi's skills and abilities. She'd noticed bigger differences in the other half, like the rustic counter that looked like a vertically cut tree. This space held more of the old charm, and so much promise. It reminded her of her *daed*'s home. She wanted to slip off her shoes and feel the old hardwood against her bare feet, to see if the childhood memories sparked by this place were as vivid as she recalled. She made a quarter turn and noticed the stacks of boxes and what looked like carpentry tools. Random items like a cookstove, pots, rolling pins, a treadle sewing machine, which she thought might be Esther's, a waist-high worktable suitable for cutting fabric, and a few other things she didn't recognize filled the space. She squinted and leaned forward to gain a better look. "Is that a horse?"

Esther chuckled. "It is. It's a piece from a carousel. Don't tell him I said it, but that nephew of mine can be too kind when it comes to payment for his jobs."

"You're telling me someone paid him with a carousel horse?"

"Sure did."

April worried her bottom lip. That almost sounded like something David would have done. Did lack of sense run in the family? She nearly snorted. She was the one who'd packed a suitcase and traveled across Kansas for a promise. A promise that may or may not bear fruit by the looks of it. Was this another bout of Esther's confusion? No, the older woman had been clear of mind since they'd crossed the threshold, leaving April to marvel at how sure Esther was of her words. She didn't pause between them or search for them. She even held a sparkle in her eyes that hadn't been there earlier. That meant Malachi had accepted payment for a job in the form of a carousel horse.

Had April imagined Esther's earlier confusion? She didn't think so. "You said this place was Malachi's, but you also said it was yours."

Nervous laughter filtered in the air. "It used to be mine, when my boys were young."

"Your boys?" April didn't hide the surprise. She remembered David talking about the great aunt who had never married.

"*Jah.* I forget. I think of Malachi and his brother Jared as my boys. I raised them after their *mamm* died."

"Oh," she said. It's all she could say. She rubbed her belly, thankful for another chance to be a mother, yet something in her yearned to offer Malachi more than condolences. What had it been like to lose his mother at such a young age? But she knew. She'd lost hers, too. At least she had her *daed* and Millie. Where had Malachi's *daed* been, leaving him with an aunt who'd never been a mother?

"Sometimes the eighty years before my last year overtake my mind and I forget time. It's a blessing to reach an old age."

Not knowing how to respond, April released her grip from the stroller and wandered to one of the bookshelves coated in several layers of dust and various knickknacks.

"It's a mess," Esther said, as if she were speaking to Jeb.

A quick glance over her shoulder told April that Esther hadn't moved, and Jeb was still sound asleep, before she turned back to try to take the "mess" all in. The difference between the two rooms was striking, as atypical as night and day, as if two unique men had maintained the same house.

"Once Malachi removes his tools, it won't be so bad. This house used to belong to his *grossdaddi*, but now it belongs to Malachi."

This bit was spoken as if Esther hadn't already told her.

"My *bruder* is Malachi's *grossdaddi*, and he built me a little place out back so I would be close to family. It was the first home my *bruder* built. Come along."

"Should we lock up while we're gone?"

"No. People around here are good neighbors and watch out for one another."

Looking at the door dividing the two storefronts, April considered grabbing her suitcase and bringing it with her. Surely, she could manage it and push the stroller, but she didn't want Esther to think she didn't trust her word.

April walked over the worn hardwood floors toward the stroller and grasped the handle. She followed behind Esther, thinking about all she'd discovered about the man who had her future in his hands. It wasn't much, but what she saw confused her as to what type of man he was, and she'd had enough of confusion and chaos to last her to her dying breath.

Was Esther right? Would Malachi relent and let her use the storefront, or would he expect her to go back to Haven? Was he strong and responsible, like her father, or was he flighty and aloof, like David had been? Or was Malachi someone else altogether?

The *boppli* kicked her stomach, thrusting April from her thoughts. She nearly laughed at how her attempt to analyze Malachi fell flat. And, for good reason—he wasn't a prospective husband. He was just a man. A man who didn't want a wife. And she was just a woman who didn't want to get married again. Not now. Not so soon after David's death. Not so close to nearly gaining her dream of owning a business. Maybe never. Still, Malachi had her future in his hands, and it would be good to know the sort of man she might strike a business deal with.

She drew in a quick breath and released it when the *boppli* shoved a foot against her rib. *Sorry, little one. I need to breathe, too.* The more she thought about Malachi and his determination to keep her from renting the storefront, the more she needed to breathe. She just wished she knew him better and knew how to convince him she would make a good tenant. But she didn't even know if he believed women could work outside the home or if, like David, he thought women had no place outside the home.

Malachi was an oxymoron, if the condition of his properties were any sign, and she wasn't sure whether or not that was a good thing. Her late husband had blown with the wind. His likes and dislikes depended always on his moods and latest obsessions. If he heard one man in their community talk about farming goats, David bought them. Whether he knew what sort of goats he was buying or not.

Turned out there was a big difference between Boer goats and milk goats. April had spent too many days rounding up wayward goats from her flower beds and their garden, as well as their *Englischer* neighbor's crops. Unfortunately, her efforts had been too little too late, and John Hathaway hadn't been too keen on the damage done. She, David, and the goats had become a source of laughter for a time after that. She hadn't blamed the community. If she hadn't been in the middle of two red-faced, blustery men, she might have laughed, too. Especially since one goat had ended up tangled in a pair of John Hathaway's overalls, and another wore Eunice Hathaway's straw hat around its neck like a prized bow.

That hadn't been the only time David's flighty tendencies had left them apologizing, embarrassed, and in a lurch, but it had been the most alarming and frightening for her.

David had wanted to be a *gut* husband. She was for sure and certain about that. And she'd loved him for trying. He just hadn't known how. Was his cousin like

David? If Malachi agreed to let her rent the storefront, would he change his mind later? Would she have to worry about eccentric items like the carousel horse showing up because he didn't know how to accept proper forms of payment for services rendered?

If she had any other choice, she'd forget about the shop and Malachi Stoltzfus. But she didn't. And now that she'd seen it with her own eyes, she wanted it even more. She squeezed her eyes closed, praying that wasn't a sin.

Please, Gotte, let this be Your will. If it isn't, I'll be content with what Your will is for me and my boppli. But if You can find it in Your heart, can I please have my own store, right there next to Malachi's place of business? I won't bother him much, and I'll even offer to keep that old carousel horse.

Chaucer, his dappled-gray half mule, half draft horse, changed pace the moment his hooves left the dusty gravel road and hit the paved surface. Malachi couldn't help smiling. Chaucer knew him too well. It was as if Chaucer understood Malachi's reluctance to return home to Esther's scheming to buy him a wife.

Malachi rolled his shoulders, attempting to relieve the knots that had taken up residence the moment he'd realized his aunt's intentions for him and April. That was the biggest reason he would not, absolutely could not, allow April to rent the storefront. She needed him. Well, not him, but she needed someone to step in and take care of her. And if he let her rent the store, she'd need him to fix something or hang something, or move something. Everyday. He already had his hands full with Esther and Jeb. If he agreed to let April rent the store, he'd soon be at her beck and call and not managing his bustling business. If he let her rent the store, Malachi wasn't sure he had it in him to utter the word *no.* At least not once he got to know someone, or felt they were somehow under his responsibility.

He scratched the side of his bare jaw and contemplated his role in April's life. Until today, she'd been nothing more than a distant relative he sent money to, to help in her time of need. Until today, she hadn't been his responsibility. Not beyond the self-imposed financial obligation he'd set upon. She was just his cousin's widow, and he'd like to keep it that way. Besides, she needed a husband, not a landlord. He laughed out loud. April had made it clear she didn't want a husband, and in her defense, she was still in her mourning period. Yet, her condition made her situation unique. He couldn't argue with Aunt Esther's logic. April needed a husband. Just not him.

Chaucer turned down a shady lane lined with frame homes. Two more turns and they'd be back at the shop. Back to Aunt Esther. Back to April. And back to the dilemma weighing down his shoulders. How would he tell her no with a finality she understood?

A groan rattled from the pit of his stomach, up his throat and through his teeth. He'd do just about anything for his cousin's widow. After all, it was his familial duty, his responsibility—but he couldn't do what Aunt Esther asked of him, adding another responsibility to his home and his name. Two responsibilities, given

April's condition. Aunt Esther, with her aging faster than he'd like to admit, and little Jeb made his proverbial plate full. And as the oldest brother, he'd already failed once. More than once, given *Mamm* blamed him for their father's departure, too. He was thankful *Mamm* hadn't witnessed Jared's misadventures. Although he was sure she would have loved Jeb. The *boppli* might have even pulled her out of bed a few times. The baby sure did that for him.

Malachi went to bed every night pondering all the what-ifs he should have handled where his younger brother was concerned and thanking *Gotte* that Jeb had made it through another day without mishap or illness. He woke up every morning praying this day would not be the day he would fail his nephew or Esther. He shuddered at the heavy awareness racing down his spine. Aunt Esther's failing health was not something he could prevent. All he could do was support her in the ways she needed, allowing her independence while she still had that ability to make her own choices. Adding two more humans to his daily routine only upped the potential of his failure. And that was unacceptable.

The reins shifted in his hands, and he realized the buggy had come to a complete stop. Chaucer hooved impatiently at the bare patch of ground near the back door of the shop. Malachi adjusted his hat and drew in an elongated breath as he buried his head into his hands.

What was he going to do about April? If Aunt Esther had her way, he'd be married by the end of the day. But that wasn't an option. Allowing April to rent the shop for her own business would only leave him feeling overly responsible for her. But he couldn't let her go back to Haven, where he assumed she had nothing left to go back to, could he? If he remembered correctly, she'd married David out of convenience and not out of love, which made him wonder if she had family at all.

He couldn't send her away, but what about a place for her to stay? There were rooms above his office and the empty storefront but the aging stairs weren't as safe as they could be, especially for a woman in her condition. And Aunt Esther's place was just too crowded.

"Hello, Malachi."

Malachi lifted his head from between his hands and eyed Aunt Esther's *Englischer* neighbor to the west side. "Hello, Mr. Gene. How are you on this fine day?"

Mr. Gene's smile didn't reach his eyes, and Malachi waited with dread for him to speak his grievances. The older man glanced toward the back of Aunt Esther's home, then toward the manicured row of red, pink, and white roses. Malachi's gut knotted. Had Aunt Esther cut more blooms from Mr. Gene's prized bushes? Malachi's teeth clenched tight.

"I don't mean to bother you, Malachi, but Aunt Esther…well, she didn't just cut a perfect rose this time, she's pruned an entire bush."

The nervous tension locking his shoulders deflated like a popped balloon. Pruning couldn't be so bad, could it? Was Mr. Gene about to thank Aunt Esther for the work?

"I know you've tried speaking to her, but it's not enough. She's cut it to the ground and had started hacking away at another before Dexter alerted me."

Malachi cringed. Dexter was a yipping little dachshund who was becoming a thorn in his side with all his tattle-telling on Aunt Esther. Nothing to be done about it, though, as it seemed Dexter was here to stay, right along with Mr. Gene. Settling his hat back on his head, Malachi climbed down from the buggy, his head bowed to hide his heated cheeks. "I'm sorry, Mr. Gene. You know, she took care of the yard for her brother for years before he passed. It is difficult for her to remember the yard is no longer her responsibility."

Mr. Gene shook his head. "I agree, it is a difficult situation, and if she'd cut them during the appropriate time of the year, I wouldn't have mentioned it, but it's early fall, too early for cutting them back. I'm afraid she's ruined them for next year. How am I to win yard of the year if she keeps destroying my flowers?"

A tinge of metal swabbed against Malachi's cheek with the nip of his teeth. "I'm sorry, Mr. Gene. I'll speak with her again."

A look of pity filled Mr. Gene's eyes. "Maybe it's time you think about getting a sitter for her. Maybe she's ready for an assisted nursing facility. We sent my mom to one last year, and she's thriving, socially. Not to mention her daily care is no longer my worry."

Malachi jerked his head up at that. Amish didn't put their elderly in homes. They kept them, moved them into their homes, and cared for them. Malachi rolled his neck. He lived with Jeb in a small farmhouse half a mile south of town. He'd begun working on renovating the place to baby-proof it, but it was small, and the only bedrooms were upstairs—stairs Aunt Esther couldn't navigate, even with his help. He could always build an addition, but that would take time. Time he didn't have. He cleared the emotion from his throat and gave Mr. Gene a considering look. Was it time to steal more of Esther's freedoms from her? Did she really need a babysitter, a nanny of sorts, like Jeb required? "It is not our way, Mr. Gene."

"There has to be a solution, Malachi. Your aunt cannot keep going on like this. It's not just about my roses. What about her safety? What if she forgets the stove is hot and touches it? What if she forgets she's cooking and catches the kitchen on fire?"

Fear struck Malachi's heart. Could she cause harm to herself?

"I'm not being dramatic, Malachi. These are real possibilities. When my mother cooked a can of cat food in the microwave, we knew it was time to look for alternatives."

"Thank you for your concern, Mr. Gene, but I don't want to force Aunt Esther from her home."

"I'm not saying an assisted living is your only option, but you need to consider some alternatives. You're a busy man with a business and a small child. You can't do this all on your own."

An image of a petite redhead with an overly round belly flashed through his mind.

Esther had brought her here for a purpose, to be his wife, and Malachi was far from agreeable to that idea. But what if *Gotte* had something else in mind? Could he convince April to care for Aunt Esther in his absence? Would giving her a purpose and a way to support herself and her coming *boppli* be enough to satisfy her? Would she forget about renting the vacant storefront? She'd seemed singularly focused and determined to rent the storefront. She'd given him reasons he should rent it to her but, he wondered, was it really about the store or was it about having a way to support herself? Certainly, it was more about her needing a place to stay for a while until she found a suitable husband to care for her and the child.

The discarded rose petals blanketing the manicured, bright green grass drew Malachi's attention. What if April declined the offer? He'd still have the dilemma of what to do with Aunt Esther. Maybe his cousin Abe and his new wife would take her. An image of Abe's new family pressed into his thoughts, and he quickly discarded that option. Abe had a farm, seven *kinder* and a new *boppli.* Abe didn't need to take on Aunt Esther, too. Besides, even though there were several nieces and nephews, Aunt Esther was his responsibility. Solely. She'd raised him and his brother when they'd needed a *mamm.* She'd taken on two little boys when she could have easily given them to another family or sent them to distant relatives. For that, he'd do anything for her.

"I don't know, Mr. Gene," Malachi said. "I may not have a choice."

In his way of thinking, April solved his problem with Aunt Esther, and Aunt Esther solved April's problem of needing a place to stay and a way to support herself and the *boppli.* He scratched his jaw and contemplated April's probable reaction, seeing her sparkling green eyes flash in irritation. He wasn't sure how April would take his offer, even if she cared to listen once he said no about the storefront. And he was quite certain Aunt Esther wouldn't accept a nanny for herself.

One thing was certain: At least Malachi would be off the hook where his responsibilities for April were concerned. Laughter pressed against his insides, but he kept it in check so Mr. Gene didn't think his mind was as scattered as Aunt Esther's had proven to be as of late. How could he think April wasn't his responsibility? She was still his kin through marriage, and in need, and he couldn't allow her to fend for herself. At least not until she was married again. Wasn't it commanded of him by *Gotte*'s word, as it said pure religion was to care for widows and orphans? Yes, ironically, hadn't he read that in James, chapter one, verse twenty-seven, only last night?

"Are you a man of faith, Mr. Gene?"

The older man pulled back his shoulders and smiled. "Strange, you ask, but yes, I am. Very much so. I go to church every Sunday."

"What do you think the Bible meant by saying, 'Pure religion and undefiled before *God* and the Father is this, To visit the fatherless and widows in their affliction, and to keep himself unspotted from the world'?"

Mr. Gene rocked on his heels and cleared his throat. "Well, I suppose it means to take care of the fatherless and the widows."

When Malachi had read that scripture last night, he'd focused on the last portion of that verse, wondering how he could keep himself from being unspotted by the world when so much of the world had infiltrated his family since he'd been a child. His father, his mother and Jared. Most bits and pieces not his doing. His father had been a sinful man. His mother confused. Yet, he and his brother had carried the burden of their choices. Malachi had prayed last night that the taint of the world would not touch Jeb. But now he saw the rest of the scripture. Pure religion was to care for the fatherless and the widows. To care for April and her *boppli*.

Mr. Gene shifted, pulling Malachi from his thoughts. "Why do you ask? Son—" Mr. Gene reached out and touched his shoulder.

Malachi searched the man's eyes for any hint of anger or displeasure, but he didn't see any and let the man continue.

"—I do not hope you think that scripture commands you to care for Esther when her needs are more than you can give, especially when you have a baby and a business. You can't watch Esther at all times, not when you live in separate homes."

Malachi pulled in a breath of air. Warm temps reminded him of spring, but the hint of decay from fallen leaves said fall was upon them. The seasons were changing the guard, and Malachi sensed his life was about to change in more ways than he liked. But hadn't he just had a big change with Jeb being dropped on his doorstep?

"Thank you, Mr. Gene, but it just isn't our way."

If he made April an offer, it didn't mean she would take it. She could make her own choice, but would his conscience be appeased if she chose not to stay in Garnett if he didn't offer her the store to rent? Would he lose sleep over her on that decision? He couldn't, because the last thing he could do was give her the shop space and be in close proximity daily. And that's what would happen because the shop needed just as much care as Esther did. It needed things fixed that a woman who was swollen with a baby couldn't do.

Having April remain in Garnett to care for Aunt Esther would solve all their problems. His aunt would be safe, April would have a roof over her head, once he convinced Aunt Esther to let him clean out one of the rooms in her home, and Malachi could keep pressing on with his life without April constantly under his foot like she would be if she made her place of business next door.

Caring for Aunt Esther wasn't the same as April renting the storefront, was it? He wouldn't see her often and he wouldn't be responsible for every repair that needed to be done on a dilapidated building with a leaky roof. She would be at Aunt Esther's house, keeping the older woman from butchering the neighbor's prize roses. He would be at his office space, at home or working on a job site. Their only interaction would be the weekly Wednesday meals Aunt Esther requested with him, and church services. The services, of course, wouldn't matter, given he didn't attend much anymore. And when he went, he rarely spoke with anyone and never stayed for dinner afterward, which would make avoiding April easy to do. Malachi didn't mind gathering with the community, but it was best for him and Jeb to keep to themselves, more than ever following Jared's latest shenanigans—Jeb was a huge reminder of all his brother had done.

"I understand, Malachi," Mr. Gene said. "Me and my wife still work, but if you want help, we'd be willing to come up with a solution. Maybe a younger woman from your community would care for Esther and your little one while you work."

"Thank you, Mr. Gene." Malachi drew in a long pull of the fall-scented air and sensed the weight of worry and guilt roll off his shoulders as he smiled to himself. Mr. Gene had given words to Malachi's thoughts. Problems solved. He could do his duty to Aunt Esther, and to his late cousin's wife—and without wedding her. The only thing left to do was to find Jeb another caretaker while he worked. But what if April was willing to care for Jeb, too? Would that be too much to ask of her? "I believe you may have offered us all a solution."

Chapter Three

With a lighter hitch in his step and less tension in his shoulders, Malachi searched his place of business and the adjoining one for April, Esther and Jeb. The extra storefront used for storage was a mess. Boxes and miscellaneous items were stacked everywhere. April seemed set on making it her own, but she didn't know what she'd asked of him. It wasn't just the store; it was the things in it. Things he'd shoved to the side, much like many of the memories he didn't want to recall.

He was glad to find the space void of humans, and quickly left the cold, gray area filled with memories of his past. Malachi strolled across the alleyway separating the properties. The line between Mr. Gene's freshly cut, bright green lawn and Aunt Esther's longer grass drew his attention. Malachi had been so busy with work and Jeb that he'd forgotten about cutting his aunt's grass. The lawn brushed over the tops of his boots, and he couldn't help wondering if Esther had set out to prune the roses because he'd shirked his duty to keep her yard manicured the way she liked it.

Stopping his stride, he glanced around, noting the apple tree was ready for picking. And then he saw the bright red leaves poking through Aunt Esther's favorite redbud. Poison ivy. How long had it been since he'd groomed his aunt's lawn? Too long if poison ivy had grown enough to choke out some branches. The last thing he needed was for her to *prune* the redbud tree and end up with a bad rash. He grunted and dipped into the small shed in Aunt Esther's backyard, pulled out a pair of heavy work gloves and took a pair of shears from the wall. He found the spray bottle filled with vinegar and a trash bag before heading toward the unwanted weed.

After laying everything down on the grass, he propped his hands on his hips as he took in the swath of seeds and leaves protruding from all directions of the redbud. Aunt Esther had planted honeysuckle one year, claiming it gave off a sweet, tantalizing aroma, of which Malachi couldn't argue, but he'd spent more hours than he cared to admit tending to the area Esther had set apart for the plant. Now, it, too, had overtaken parts of Esther's redbud tree and peonies. The honeysuckle reached nearly ten feet outside of the small latticework Aunt Esther had designated as the honeysuckle's home. Poison ivy wove around every branch, growing upward and outward. He itched just looking at the bright red leaves surrounding the redbud and the honeysuckle. It was a good reminder of just how much Malachi had neglected his duty to Aunt Esther.

Thankfully, Mr. Gene hadn't fussed about the grass or the poison ivy. And, thankfully, Bishop Mueller hadn't paid Malachi a visit either. If Mr. Gene had opted to go to the bishop instead of speaking with Malachi because the previous times hadn't worked, it wouldn't have boded well. A visit from the bishop would cause speculation as well as additional gossip and suspicion that Malachi was more like his wastrel father than anyone realized. Not that the community had outright said such things to his face, but he'd heard whispers as a child, and those whispers had clawed at his ears and thoughts for many years.

Malachi cringed and promised himself that he'd do better. For Aunt Esther, Jeb, and now for April and her *boppli.* At least until she found a new husband. Offering April a temporary position taking care of Aunt Esther, was a start. He only hoped she'd take it.

He yanked on the work gloves with more force than necessary and turned to face the back of the building he used as a place of business and the building attached. The shop needed work. A lot of work. It had needed work when Aunt Esther had used the space, and it'd been too difficult for Malachi to cross the threshold with an eye to inspection and detail, so Jared had helped their aunt with the repairs when they came up. Even though many years had passed, every time Malachi entered the adjoining store, he expected to see his *mamm* sitting at her sewing machine or laughing with a customer. He'd refurbished the adjoining doors before beginning working there just so he wouldn't have to think about the times when his *mamm* had refused to leave her bed, leaving Malachi to deal with the customers, making her excuses when she didn't fill orders on time.

Could he enter the old sewing shop without experiencing impending doom? Yeah, if he was only shoving boxes in the corners or looking for a petite redhead with sparkling green eyes. But to go in and spend more minutes than he could hold his breath? That would be impossible. If forced to spend more time than he was willing, he feared he'd follow his mother's path. And he couldn't. He had Jeb to consider. He had Aunt Esther and his customers. He wouldn't let them down.

Determined to deny April's request, but to offer her a place as Aunt Esther's nurse, he shrugged off the old sewing shop and turned back to the yard work at hand. He almost laughed to himself as he wondered if he could save the honeysuckle and the redbud. The poison ivy sought to squeeze the life out of the pair, just like the sewing shop threatened to choke the life out of him. If only cutting back vines and pouring vinegar on the roots would remove the memories of his childhood. Could he salvage the tree and bush? He wasn't sure, but he had to try for his great aunt's sake.

By the time he treated the last root with vinegar, the sun was losing its strength, and it was past time he should have gathered Jeb and gone home for dinner. After putting everything away and cleaning up, he snagged a basket and filled it with apples. He smiled at his harvest. This would make Aunt Esther happy, and her apple pies would make his stomach happy.

He eased open the screen door to her kitchen. Malachi ducked beneath the door frame and focused on his plan of action as he settled the basket on the small roll-away butcher-block counter he'd made so Aunt Esther could move it around. He hadn't expected to be greeted with such a delicious smell, which immediately caused his stomach to race into starvation mode and grumble at the lack of sustenance he'd had that day. It wasn't Aunt Esther's typical fare of egg salad sandwiches and a bowl of soup they shared on Wednesdays. How long had it been since he'd had a really good homemade meal? Since the Sunday service? No, he'd missed that one out of fear little Jeb would catch a cold in the rain. He shucked off his boots and left them where they lay.

"Aunt Esther," he called as he stalked toward the living room. Aunt Esther's home was an open space, with the living room visible from the kitchen. "Dinner smells good."

"Shhhhh!" Aunt Esther motioned with her finger at the wooden rocking chair in the corner by the small dining table. Malachi stopped dead in his tracks. He waited for the blood to resume its flow in his veins before he considered the scene before him. April sat on the rocker he'd made solely for rocking Jeb whenever he visited his aunt. April's head leaned back against the headrest, cushioned with a couch pillow, another squished between the lathed rungs and the curve of her back. Jeb's little limbs curled around her as if they were one being. His soft, downy head snuggled against her neck. It was a beautiful sight. He couldn't shake the idea that this should be one of those perfect moments to brand in his mind, but it wasn't. April wasn't his wife, and she wasn't holding their sleeping child. She wasn't even holding *his* child. She was holding his nephew. A little boy with an unknown mother and a wayward father. An orphan. Still, he loved the *boppli* as if he were his own.

He shook his head. That wasn't true. Jeb was his

son, just not through the normal course of nature. His by heart. And that curious woman held him as if he was the most precious thing in the world, which set Malachi at odds with *Gotte,* given Jeb's own parents hadn't considered him precious enough to stick around. To see April cuddle Jeb and hold him in such a caring and loving manner stirred an ache deep in his chest.

He rubbed at the pain, wishing it would go away. He'd long ago given up on ever having a normal family. A *fraa* and *bopplis* of his own. What woman would want to marry him with the taint of his *daed*'s reputation and now his brother's? It didn't matter, though. He had Jeb, even if only for a short time, and he'd make the best of it while he could. Still, he couldn't help wondering that if April was this loving to a stranger's child... How would she be with her own? How would she be with one of theirs?

He dropped his knuckles from his chest and cleared his throat at the intrusive thought. April hadn't even been there a day, and she was stirring thoughts in his mind that he had no right thinking. That made it even more important for him to convince her to forget about the store.

"As it should be, ain't so?" Aunt Esther's whisper might as well have rung through one of those loudspeakers at a high school football game, for all the startle it gave him. "My house hasn't smelled this good since you and Jared were in school."

That was about the time they'd both started working and were rarely home with their aunt. Malachi had found a piece of land farther outside of town and built his own small house, big enough for him and a dog if he ever wanted, and Jared had run off, leaving Aunt Esther to live alone. Cooking for one hadn't been worth the effort, so instead she'd baked bread and ate sandwiches.

"She'd make Jeb a *gut mamm, jah*?"

Malachi crossed his arms, and even though he couldn't really argue with her, since Jeb should have a mother, he glared at Aunt Esther. "No matter what's going on in that head of yours, Esther Beiler, it isn't happening. No way, no how, am I marrying that woman." Or any woman.

"Shush, now," Aunt Esther said, pointedly glancing at the sleeping duo. "You'll wake them."

He lowered his voice and hunched closer to her ear. "If I didn't have a solution to you inviting her here for no good reason, I'd send her back. But seems like you've been causing trouble with the neighbors again, and April just may curb your stubborn tendencies. If she agrees."

"Now, you wait a minute. I've done nothing wrong to anyone," she said before adding, "or anything."

"Oh? You didn't cut Mr. Gene's rosebushes, today?" He emphasized with an eyebrow.

She turned away from him, but he noticed the high rosy color of her cheeks before she did. Aunt Esther took up a knife and began slicing a loaf of freshly baked bread. "Maybe I did, Malachi, but those nasty Japanese beetles were eating the petals."

At least she thought she'd had a good reason. Malachi touched her shoulder and softened his tone. "Aunt Esther, the roses aren't your responsibility anymore.

We should be happy Mr. Gene hasn't gone to the bishop about your unwillingness to heed his wishes. It isn't your home, and it isn't your brother's home either. It is Mr. Gene's, and those are his roses."

She dropped her chin to her chest, and Malachi felt her defeat in the center of his own. He hadn't meant to sound harsh or to be stern with her, but she needed to understand she couldn't cut the man's roses whenever she wanted. Malachi clenched his free hand into a tight fist. He disliked these talks, almost as much as he was sure she did.

"I may have forgotten for a moment," she said. "I know he wasn't happy."

Wasn't happy? Malachi stopped himself from raising his voice, but the urge to yell shook him. That had been his *daed*'s way whenever he became angry. Malachi wasn't mad. Only frustrated. He disliked any confrontation and did everything he could to avoid it, even when it was necessary. That was one reason he had a carousel horse in the storeroom, among other useless items. Confrontation frightened him. Becoming like his father terrified him even more. His jaw clenched as he swallowed the rising anxiousness. It wasn't Esther's fault. She couldn't help the slips of her mind. But if April didn't agree to his solution, he feared Mr. Gene might take matters into his own hands. "I'd say Mr. Gene was less than happy, Aunt Esther. He suggested I put you in one of those homes where the *Englischers* send their old people."

She sucked air in so fast, she sputtered.

Malachi rubbed circles on her back until she calmed.

"Don't worry, it's not our way. Even if it were, it's not mine. Besides, you didn't throw Jared and me out on our ears when we acted up. You gave us warm beds and filled our stomachs. I won't toss you out either."

Aunt Esther wrapped her arms around his middle and looked up at him with clear, bright eyes. "You're a *gut* boy, Malachi. I only want what's best for you and Jeb." She pulled back and turned a worried expression toward April. Like a bee to pollen, Malachi's gaze followed. "She's a *gut* woman, too, and been through more than one so young should. Give her a chance, Malachi, for me."

Releasing Aunt Esther, he walked toward the window, looking out at the backyard. He had no doubt April was a good Amish woman and would make a *wunderbar mamm*, but what his aunt intended was impossible. Malachi wouldn't marry and live under suspicion with a *fraa*, with no trust between them. That's how it'd been with his parents. He'd lived under the shame and speculation of their community. Leaning against the window frame, he motioned toward the yard. "I trimmed the redbud and found a poison ivy bush swallowing it and your honeysuckle. I think I saved it."

"I hope the apples weren't ruined."

He blinked, thinking maybe Aunt Esther was confused by which tree he'd said had been confined by the ivy. They'd had a trying enough day as it was, so Malachi chose not to correct her. "They don't appear to be. I brought a basket full of apples in and sat them on the counter. They're ready for pie making."

"Pssh," she said, smacking his arm. "Mark my words, Malachi, you won't have apple pie until you take a wife."

Malachi rolled his eyes and was about to reaffirm his stance on remaining single when Jeb whimpered. He spun on his wool-clad heel and found a pair of mossy green eyes watching him.

April wasn't sure what had pulled her from a deep sleep, but once she realized the weight against her chest was a real infant, and not the constant fear of the unknown, she remembered she was in Garnett, where she'd followed a ray of hope only to have it darkened with a large gray cloud, otherwise known as Malachi.

She hadn't intended on eavesdropping, and in her defense, the exchange between Esther and her great nephew had been nothing more than conversation. Until Esther had mentioned marriage. Again. April did not want to hear any more rejections from him, or the reasons he wouldn't marry her. She was certain she had more reasons than he did. The only difference, if he didn't allow her to rent the storefront, was that she'd be left with little choice but to fall on the mercy of a single Amish man, especially because she carried her own *boppli*, and probably couldn't return to Haven.

She shifted Jeb's weight to give her arm some relief from the tingling, only to have the *boppli* alert Malachi to her being awake. Her eyes grew wide at the arching of Malachi's dark eyebrow. She patted Jeb's bottom and smiled. Should she pretend as if she hadn't heard a word?

No.

She arched her back and opened her eyes.

"I hope whomever you marry makes apple pie as good as I do," April said. "I couldn't make them fast enough in Haven." That was the truth. She'd received a lot of orders for her pies and other baked goods from the surrounding communities, but that wasn't all she'd wanted to sell at her store once Malachi relented. Maybe that carousel horse. She nearly laughed out loud at her inside joke but stopped herself. She wouldn't touch the large ornamental object, but she had intended to make homemade candles and scented soaps. She'd also planned to bring in items from other women in the community. "It's one product I hope to sell in my store."

She'd hoped to sway his stomach with the lure of sweets, but the narrowing of his eyes told her he wasn't buying. She'd have to find another tactic.

"No matter," she said. She scooted forward in the rocker and planted her feet on the floor. Before she could heft herself out of the chair, Malachi was beside her, relieving her of Jeb's weight while assisting her to an upright position. She stretched her back, then rubbed her palm over her stomach. *"Denki."*

"I don't think you could sell enough apple pies to keep the business going. Aunt Esther doesn't have enough trees to supply you with a sufficient amount of apples."

She scowled. "Of course not. I'll have to expand on other baked goods and supplies, as well as—"

Jeb wailed. April took him from Malachi's arms and began bouncing him until he settled.

"She has a way with Jeb," Esther said as she shuffled to the stove.

Malachi tucked his thumbs behind his suspenders. His expression was unreadable, but if she had to guess, April imagined he was trying to find another way to tell his aunt he wasn't going to marry. After spending much of the day with Esther, she had concluded the older woman didn't pay attention to anything else once she set her mind on something. But April could be stubborn, and she had a feeling Malachi held his own streak of the trait as well.

April dipped her head and nuzzled Jeb's neck. "I'm sorry for taking him from you like that. It's a habit, I suppose. David never took to our *boppli*."

He hadn't even held Samantha.

With a shake of his head, Malachi rubbed his palm against Jeb's back. "No need to apologize. It's kind of nice not to feel a sense of urgency when he cries. He does likes you."

"Denki." She kissed the top of the *boppli*'s head. "I like him, too."

A loud rumble broke the silence between them. April giggled. "All this talk about pie has you hungry."

A smile spread over Malachi's face, softening the rock-hardness of his jaw, and for a moment she saw him without the barriers he erected. "Combined with the delicious smell of food and the fact I missed lunch, I'd say my stomach has a right to be hungry."

"Well, I suppose so. Good thing there is enough to feed the town," April said.

He leaned closer, as if to tell her a secret, but he kept

his voice level. "It's not often Aunt Esther cooks," he said, winking. "So, I thank you for being the cause."

"Oh," Esther said as she set a casserole dish onto the table. "I didn't cook. April did."

Malachi swung his gaze to meet hers. Shock and wonder.

She might have made the casserole, the loaf of bread and a peach cobbler, but she felt like his aunt was about to serve her up on a platter for Malachi, and he didn't realize it. He stood there, mouth agape, as if waiting to be spoon fed. Esther had set a trap for Malachi, using April's cooking as bait, and they both had walked right into it. She stifled the urge to groan at the older woman's matchmaking schemes.

But April had other plans. If he saw her value, maybe he wouldn't be so hard-pressed to send her away. She shifted her weight and scooted around Malachi. She needed space and to keep from looking at him. He was too easy to tease and talk to, which was out of character for her, especially after living with David. The carefree woman she'd once been had disappeared upon her nuptials, but she was finding glimpses of her old self with this man, proving Malachi was nothing like David.

If she didn't watch herself, and Esther, there'd be a wedding before she knew it.

Hers and Malachi's.

But it wouldn't work. She'd been married once and didn't relish the thought of entering that institution again if she didn't have to. Marriage afforded her little freedom. None actually. And she wasn't too keen on losing the freedoms she had gained since David's death.

That was why the success of the store was so important. She needed to find herself again, and the store was the only way she saw of accomplishing that goal.

First, she had to convince Malachi to let her have the space to rent. Maybe if he liked her cooking enough, she could bargain with him. And after what she'd seen in the vacant store, Malachi liked to barter. She couldn't offer him a carousel horse, but daily meals, plus rent for the store, should suffice. Of course, she wouldn't mind keeping little Jeb, too, if he allowed her to.

She laid the baby in the bassinet next to the table and then dished a heaping spoonful of the casserole onto Malachi's plate, onto Esther's, and then onto hers. She scooted into the empty chair, and they all bowed their heads in silence. April wasn't sure what the others prayed, outside being thankful for the meal, but she prayed running her own store was in *Gotte*'s will for her and her *boppli.*

"This looks delicious." Malachi's stomach agreed and Esther laughed.

"A wife would see to it you never went without a meal," Esther said.

April chewed the inside of her cheek. When she'd left Haven, behind, she'd thought she'd left the push for marriage, too.

"Aunt Esther, please. I'm not in need of a wife, nor am I in want of one."

Relief eased through April's shoulders. At least she and Malachi were of the same mind about marriage. Now, if only she could convince him to let her stay in Garnett and make a go of her own store.

"Sometimes," Esther said, "we don't know what we want or need."

Malachi scrubbed his palm over his bare face, and April had to admit he was handsome. He was easy on the eyes, and she could imagine herself sitting across from him at the kitchen table as they drank their morning coffee. Something she and David never had done. He'd never lingered over breakfast, always snagging his dish from the table as he'd run out the door.

"I'll admit I'm in need of help," Malachi said with his fork in midair.

This drew April's interest, and she found herself staring into his dark blue eyes as he held her gaze. She moistened her lips in hopeful anticipation. The *boppli* rolled around in her womb as if sensing her excitement. Had Malachi changed his mind? Would he allow her to rent the storefront? She almost squealed in excitement. Her dream was finally about to come true, and no husband was going to tell her it couldn't.

Chapter Four

Malachi massaged his thighs with his palms. He looked between the two women, both with hopeful expressions. Could he speak what was on his mind in Aunt Esther's presence without upsetting her? Based upon the way she'd responded when he'd mentioned the homes where the *Englischers* sent their elderly, he didn't think so. His aunt would take offense at needing a caretaker, but Malachi didn't see that he had a choice.

He took up his fork and slid it under the casserole on his plate. Cheese dripped from the potatoes and hamburger. His mouth watered. He opened wide and was about to take a bite when April huffed. He slid his gaze toward her and raised an eyebrow in question. Her cheeks turned pink, and she quickly glanced down at her lap.

"Is there something you'd like to say?"

She shook her head. "It is none of my concern."

"Of course, it is, dear," Aunt Esther said. "You are family, and we speak our minds around here. Isn't that right, Malachi?"

He shoved the bite of casserole into his mouth. The flavor bathed his taste buds. He leaned back in his chair and closed his eyes as he chewed. If he didn't answer his aunt, would she drop it? He'd hoped she wouldn't press him further. Aunt Esther often spoke her mind. He did not. And when he did, he tried to take care with his words. He didn't want to encourage more outspokenness when he believed some things were best spoken in private. Like his need for a caretaker for his nephew and aunt.

"Well, Malachi, what do you think?" Esther's fork scraped against her plate as April sat quietly with her hands folded in her lap. He hadn't heard her shift in her chair. "Is April's cooking worthy a wife?"

He kept his growl in check. Somehow, without losing his patience, he had to convince his aunt he wasn't in need of a wife. He opened his eyes, and as he'd suspected, April hadn't moved. Her submissiveness didn't sit well in his mind. He wished she'd say something. "It is well enough."

That drew a flicker of annoyance in his direction from her. He smiled at her and tried to ease her mind. "It is delicious, April. I can't remember a meal this nice, but if you don't mind, I'd like to enjoy the meal in silence. Can we talk after dinner?"

"It is no matter to me," she said as she pushed from the table. "I'll get some more lemonade."

"No need. April, please sit and enjoy the fruits of your labor." He glanced between the two women and considered his words. He needed to reassure April without upsetting Aunt Esther. Jeb began to fuss, and April picked up the baby. "I believe our conversation can wait until after we eat, when we are not so easily distracted by fussy babies."

"You mean away from listening, meddling old ladies," Aunt Esther said.

That, too. The thought thrust into his mind like a hammer striking a nail, but he quickly halted them before they reached his mouth.

"Not exactly my intention, Aunt Esther, but a conversation would be easier without the word *wife* in every other sentence."

April laughed. "That is one thing we agree on."

She propped Jeb against her shoulder and softly crooned in his ear until he settled. It was hard not to watch her with his nephew. The sight of them together, and how easily Jeb took to April's nurturing, was mesmerizing.

"You are good with him."

Her eyes flickered in surprise. *"Denki."*

He sat forward and leaned his elbows on the table. "You're not used to compliments, are you?"

"I have had my share, but I find it odd. Aren't all women good with babies?"

He considered her question, thinking about all the women he knew with babies. Naomi, his cousin's wife, had a *boppli*, and she'd taken on the responsibility of her siblings after their parents had died when an *Englischer's* car plowed into their buggy. She had experience. Being the eldest sister of seven *bruders* and *schwesters* she had a great deal of experience. Did that make her good with babies? He had no recollections of his own mother caring for Jared, but she hadn't had the mental ability to be an attentive mother. She'd done the best she could, given the circumstances of her mental illness. He didn't fault her, and had forgiven her a long time ago, but that didn't mean he didn't wish things had been different. He glanced at the woman who'd stepped in and cared for two rambunctious boys with so much love, but she'd had no children of her own.

He gave April a pointed look. "Honestly, I wouldn't know."

"Well," April said, rising from the chair. She paced around the dining table as she bounced Jeb. "I've not met a woman who didn't have motherly instincts."

She stopped and lifted the infant into the air. Joy beamed from her as she smiled at his nephew. "Who couldn't love such a sweet, innocent child? They are gifts from *Gotte*, *jah*? Offered to us for a time to care for. They are *Gotte*'s and as such, they should be loved and cared for as *He* loves and cares for us."

This was a wisdom he hadn't considered. She'd endured much in the last year with the loss of her husband and child, but was this wisdom of hers the reason behind her fortitude? If he could take a wife, he'd be honored to marry one like her. It was a shame he would never marry, though. *Jah*, the greater shame would be if he married and subjected her to his family's tragic history. It was a good thing April wasn't in want of a husband lest he might be tempted to cross the invisible boundaries he'd set for himself.

"See," Aunt Esther said. "She'd make a *wunderbar* wife."

Malachi patted his aunt's papery hand. "I've never

questioned her ability to make a *wunderbar* wife, Aunt Esther."

April was easy on the eyes. Her pregnancy only made her more beautiful, and the fact she took so easily to Jeb made her even more appealing to Malachi's eye. It didn't hurt she'd cooked an excellent meal. He could get used to coming home every night after work to April's cooking. Jeb fussed, and she crooned in the infant's ear. A melodious song filled the room, luring his ears to attention. It was like a balm to an open wound. Both soothing and nettling, like salt.

He'd forgiven his mother, but he could not forget the melancholy she'd suffered every time his father had abandoned them. A melancholy Malachi feared he carried in his own blood. He would not risk his heart, knowing once April heard about the perils of his family, she would form an opinion. An opinion that would have her distancing herself from him, and Jeb. He would not do that to Jeb. Not like his mother had done to him and Jared.

"I am not looking for a wife, and April has made it clear she is not looking for a husband. Now, I say this with much affection for you, Aunt Esther, can we please drop the matter?" Malachi completed the last few bites on his plate and cleared the table.

"Please, don't," April said. "I will do that once this little guy is settled."

"No need," he said as he carried the dishes to the sink and settled them in the water, already prepared to clean the cooking dishes. The water remained warm, and he wondered how hot it had been when April washed the pans she'd cooked. Had the water seared her scarred hands? Had it caused her pain?

He turned and looked at April, sliding his gaze to the hands holding Jeb. They were red, but were they more red than they had been before? He couldn't be sure, but he would make a note to return from work before dinnertime to help her in the future. If she agreed to his offer. He wouldn't think about how that would have him spending more time in her company. "I've been a bachelor a long time and do not mind cleaning up after myself or anyone else."

"See," Aunt Esther said, and Malachi held his tongue, knowing she had yet to let loose the subject of marriage. "You two would make a good partnership."

"Esther." April spoke softly. "*Denki* for thinking of us so highly and believing I would make a *gut* wife for your nephew, but I am still in mourning and don't wish to think about marrying, yet."

Malachi ran a dish cloth over one plate and dunked it in the rinse water before setting it on a towel. April's excuse was valid. She was still in mourning. However, her situation was unique in that she would soon have a *boppli* to think of. How would she care for the infant without a husband to support her? He would have to thank April later for her intervention. Surely, Aunt Esther would stop pestering them. April had only arrived early today, and his aunt had pressed them at every turn. He hoped April's pleas would encourage Esther's silence on the matter.

Esther's chair creaked, and Malachi glanced over his shoulder. His aunt approached April and rested her gnarled, boney fingers against the swollen belly. "What of the baby?"

The genuine concern in Aunt Esther's tone tugged on his heart, and he knew he had to convince April to agree to his plan. He couldn't allow her to leave Garnett, because she had nowhere else to go. *Gotte* had brought April here for a reason, and even if *Gotte* had used a well-intentioned busybody with a mind to get him married, the outcome was the same. He needed April's help, and *Gotte* knew he'd need help with Esther.

He dried his hands on a towel and walked across the room. "The baby will be fine. April will be fine."

"Oh, thank goodness." Aunt Esther moistened her thin lips. "You've come to your senses."

April's beautiful eyes widened, but he couldn't tell whether it was in fear or joy. Until she shook her head. "I won't marry you."

He couldn't help it. Joy filled his chest, and he smiled. "I haven't asked you to marry me, April."

"Denki." She seemed to deflate. Her eyebrows rose as she looked up at him. "The store?"

He shook his head. "I am genuinely sorry, April. That is not something I can do."

"Can't or won't?" she asked.

Was there a difference?

"I've seen it and know all it needs is some elbow grease. If it's a matter of cleaning it out—"

"It's not."

"Malachi," Aunt Esther said. "The space isn't being used."

"It is," he said. "That is final, and I won't hear another word on the matter. Both of you, please don't push."

April buried her face into the crease of Jeb's neck. Was she hiding tears, or worse, fear, because he'd grown stern? Images of his *mamm*'s tears pressed into his mind. His *daed* hadn't always been kind, and his words often had been gruff, leaving *Mamm* crying. Malachi wished he could take back the words. No, not the words, but the frustration behind them.

"April, I am sorry, but the store is not up for discussion. Not at this time." He raked his palm over his jaw. Shadows grew over the lawn outside, and if he was going to get Jeb home before dark, they'd have to leave soon. "But I do have a proposition for you."

This drew her gaze to his. Her red-rimmed, watery-green eyes told him she'd fought back tears.

"It has come to my attention that Aunt Esther needs care," he said.

"Now, you wait a minute, Malachi Stoltzfus. I do not need sitting like a child." Aunt Esther jabbed a shaking finger in his direction.

"Maybe not sitting, Aunt Esther, but you need supervision, and before the bishop is involved." He paced to the side windows, looking out at the neighbor's home. "I think you and I can both agree, your mind isn't what it once was, and I cannot be here at all times to make sure you don't burn down the house."

His aunt's sharp breath filled the silence. "I would never!"

He turned on his heel and glanced between the two women. One held much of his heart. The other? He did not know. Both were his responsibility. "Three months ago, you wouldn't have cut the neighbor's rosebush to the ground either. Things have changed, ain't so? What about last week when I found you walking aimlessly down a dirt road? You were going to visit your sister, who died several years back." He regretted bringing up the incident at his aunt's pale face and softened his tone. "Aunt Esther, we can't ignore this any longer. If you are to stay here in your home, we need April's help." He licked his lips. "I will pay you, April, affording you the independence you wish for you and your *boppli*."

April rocked back and forth as if to soothe Jeb. However, he sensed it was more to soothe herself. Would she consider the idea, or would she say no?

"Malachi, I am not a child," Aunt Esther argued.

"No, you are not, but you are also no longer yourself all the time either." He exhaled then walked toward his aunt and wrapped his callused hand around her soft one. "You are my responsibility, and it would tear me apart if something happened to you when it could have been prevented."

She shook her head. "I don't need a babysitter."

He chewed his bottom lip and sought the right words.

"Not a babysitter." April's soft voice interrupted his thoughts. "A companion."

Did this mean April would say yes to his proposal? No, not his proposal, but his offer?

"Companion?" Aunt Esther blinked, then drew in a deep breath. She pulled her hand from his and turned her back on him.

He waited patiently for her to say something, anything, to show she would relent. He had a long day of work tomorrow, and he needed to get little Jeb home before it was too late. "Well?"

"I'll do it," April said, surprising him. "But only until I find someone willing to rent a single woman a store, so I can start my own business."

Her words kicked him in the gut, and he wished the store had never belonged to him. "Aunt Esther, what say you?"

"I say," she said, turning back, her arms crossed in mock defiance, the glint in her dulling eyes warning him she was up to more scheming. "Okay."

He raised an eyebrow. "Okay?"

"*Jah*," she said. "Are you the one losing your mind, Malachi? *Jah*."

The corners of her mouth curved upward.

His heart sank to his feet. What was she up to? "There will be no marriage, Aunt Esther, so get that out of your hard head, will you?"

Her silence was answer enough.

He massaged the tension from his neck. "I have a long day tomorrow. Jeb and I'll be going now." He addressed April, "I'm sorry I haven't found a place for you to sleep tonight, but tomorrow, when I'm done, we'll come up with something. I'm sure Aunt Esther won't mind us cleaning one of her rooms."

"Oh," April said. "We've already taken care of that."

She'd surprised him once again. "You've taken care of Jeb, cooked a delicious meal, and cleaned out one of Aunt Esther's rooms while I was gone this afternoon?"

All of that after walking to town with a heavy suitcase after her driver's car broke down?

"*Jah*," she said. "I don't like keeping my hands idle, and Jeb is such a *gut* baby, it's easy to get things done."

"I told you she'd make a *gut* wife."

Chapter Five

Birdsong danced through the cracked window and April stretched the stiffness from her limbs, sinking into the soft mattress. She rubbed the sleep from her eyes and sat up. A beautiful quilt, in muted pinks and lilacs, fell onto her lap. She breathed in and out in slow, gentle breaths to gather her thoughts from the evening before. The cool morning air woke her more effectively than a cup of black coffee, which she'd quit drinking the moment she'd realized she was carrying a *boppli*. However, the fresh air didn't settle her mind, as the worries of yesterday had carried through to today.

If Malachi wouldn't rent the store to her, how would she gain her independence? Would she always be at the mercy of another human being with little choice of her own? It didn't seem quite right in the grand scheme of things, but since it wasn't her place to force the matter, she'd let it drop. At least she had a job, one that allowed her room and board in a warm and seemingly friendly home.

The *boppli* rolled around as if in agreement. "The bed is much softer than the cot we slept on, ain't so? Still, it'd be nice to have a place of our own before you make your arrival, but I will be grateful, nonetheless, as we should be."

She dangled her feet off the edge of the mattress, her toes nowhere near touching the floor, which made her giggle. David had been a tall man, and their mattress had suited him. She'd had to use a crate she'd confiscated from the barn to get in and out of bed easily. The frame for this mattress wasn't nearly as tall, and if she shimmied a little and stretched her feet, she'd reach the floor without falling. It was a minor inconvenience, the price well worth a good night's rest. The first in as long as she could remember. And she wasn't sure if she should feel guilty or not. Maybe exhaustion from walking almost two miles into town carrying a suitcase had lulled her into a deep sleep, or maybe it had been from all the work she and Esther had done to clean up this room. Of course, it could have been the nice, soft mattress and pillow she'd slept on. It had nothing to do with her irritation at Malachi's unwillingness to rent his empty store or her worry over her future and that of her baby's.

She rubbed her palm over her stomach and reached for the salve on the bedside table. She rubbed the ointment into her hands and breathed deep of the myrrh-scented lotion. Whatever had induced the good night's sleep, she was thankful that worry over her future and that of her *boppli*'s hadn't kept her up.

She didn't want to drop the matter of the store, but maybe she should. After all, Esther had suggested another landlord with an available property might be willing to rent to a single woman. If not, April would only find another way to convince Malachi what a great tenant she would be. But the desperation in his eyes last night had tugged on her conscience. She'd seen hints of Esther's mental state but hadn't placed it until Malachi voiced it. He needed her help. Esther needed her help. And she needed theirs, too. Even if she didn't, she couldn't abandon her *boppli*'s great-aunt or her late husband's cousin. Besides, providing companionship to Esther was a chance to prove how hardworking she was, and then maybe Malachi would change his mind. All April had to do was be patient and look for opportunities to win him over.

"Not exactly what I had in mind when I traveled all this way, *Gotte*." But April would help, and be glad of it, until she figured out her next step or until Malachi relented in her quest for independence. In the meantime, she'd do all she could to convince him that she could be a profit to him and not a deficit. She'd make him see her plans for the storefront were more than a dream of a woman with little thought for anything other than cooking and cleaning. She didn't mind those things, but David had never been satisfied with her efforts, often complaining about little things like dried bits of mud on the floor from his boots after she'd just finished mopping.

April sighed and stretched her feet to reach the floor. It wouldn't do her any good to dwell on the disappointment of her previous marriage. It would only incite regret and unforgiveness toward a man who could no longer ask for understanding. Besides, her marriage had been her doing. She'd agreed to marry David only because it was time to vacate her *daed*'s home to make room for his new wife and her *kinder.* She should have taken more time to get to know him, but since she'd known no one like him who could turn from laughing to anger in a single breath, she'd been ignorant of what sort of life she'd have as David's wife. And since her parents' marriage and that of her father and his new wife were the only examples of what she thought a marriage should be like, she feared all men were not like her father, but like David, which scared her.

A soft knock tapped on her door. "April, are you awake?"

She pushed to her feet and opened the door to find Esther fully dressed and beaming. "*Jah*, just now."

"*Gut*," Esther said, rubbing her hands together. "If you're going to be my companion, we have work to do."

April felt the sting of ridicule. She wasn't lazy, but Esther's insinuation reminded her of David's displeasure. She blinked back the tears forming, but not before Esther noticed.

"Oh, dear, I meant nothing by it. It's just...well, Malachi will be at his shop before long and I want to be underfoot."

"What?" April shook her head, uncertain if she heard Esther correctly. "If I'm to be your car—companion, we better not cause any problems for Malachi."

Esther cackled. "Oh, we won't be causing problems, we'll be solving them. If I guess right, he still has found no one to keep Jeb while he works. He wanted to hire a... Hmm, what did he call them?"

"A nanny?" April suggested.

"*Jah*, that's exactly what he said. But my neighbor distracted him about those Japanese-beetle-infested roses and I'm sure he's forgotten all about his need to make plans for Jeb. You and I," Esther said, motioning between them, "are going to be there when he needs us."

"I'm not sure that's such a *gut* idea, Esther." Especially if she wanted to earn Malachi's trust. Something she'd thought about as she'd laid in bed last night waiting for sleep to come. The best plan she had for her and the *boppli* was to bide her time while caring for Esther. If Malachi got to know her and to see how hard she was willing to work, then maybe he'd allow her to rent the store. But if she was caught helping his aunt manipulate him, she'd lose all integrity in his eyes, and that was something she didn't want to risk.

Esther beamed. "It's a *wunderbar* idea. Did you see the mess he has scheduled? He's too busy to know whether he's coming or going. He'll be at a loss when he has to leave for a job."

The *boppli* rolled around in April's stomach, reminding her it was time to eat. "How about I make some breakfast for us, and then we can discuss it while we eat. I don't think showing up at Malachi's place of business is what he had in mind when he hired me to be your companion."

"Of course, it wasn't," Esther said. "My nephew doesn't know what he wants or what he needs. And he thinks I'm the one losing my mind, ain't so?"

"I don't think he said that in so many words," April said. "He's worried, and rightly so, *jah*? What if your neighbor hadn't been kind enough to wait for Malachi and confronted you instead? What if his anger had spurred him into actions that would have harmed you?"

Esther's brow wrinkled as she considered April's words. "You're a *gut* woman, April Beiler."

April clamped her teeth on her bottom lip and braced herself for Esther to bring up marriage again. Gratitude filled her when the topic didn't surface.

"I suppose breakfast would do us both some good," Esther said. "We have some time to make him see the error of his ways. You get dressed, and I'll see you in the kitchen."

April shut the door and quickly dressed before rushing downstairs into the kitchen. She half expected the elderly aunt to be absent. She was surprised to find Esther sitting at the dining table, in the glow of the lantern, staring into her black coffee, especially when she had been fully prepared to march to Malachi's office and haul Esther home.

"How about a *gut* morning to you, Esther?" April slid open the white curtains hanging above the sink. Indigo, streaked with brilliant pinks, painted the morning horizon. "The sun will soon rise."

April sat the cast iron on the warm cookstove to heat and then grabbed a few eggs from the basket on the counter and cracked them into a bowl. She added milk before whisking them with salt, pepper and paprika, then diced up a small onion and a clove of garlic. She set the bowl aside, and found some bacon in the refrigerator and laid a few pieces in the heated pan. The instant sizzle caused her stomach to grumble. She turned to check on Esther, since she hadn't responded to her good morning.

"We should go over your routine, so I know what to expect."

"Not much to it anymore," Esther said with a wistfulness that brought April a little sadness.

"What days do you bake bread? What about clothes washing and going to the store?"

"Since it's just me, I bake when I need to. Shop when I need to, except Wednesdays. I try to have fresh bread for when Malachi and Jeb come for dinner."

Esther sounded more lucid than she had yesterday with the mixed-up conversations. April did not know how long that would last. What worried her was Esther's plan to ambush Malachi with their presence at his place of business. Somehow, April needed to redirect the old woman's intentions. April flipped the bacon, and pressed it flat with her fork, pleased with the amount of grease filling the bottom of the pan. "That's good to know. What do you make for dinner?"

"Sandwiches."

That surprised April, as Malachi seemed to be a man who enjoyed the hearty meal she'd made last night. "Tomorrow is Wednesday. Are sandwiches what you would like to have, or would you like me to prepare another casserole? Maybe an apple pie?"

The worry line marring Esther's brow smoothed, and a glint twinkled in her eye. What was she thinking?

"A casserole would be *gut*. I'm certain he's tired of sandwiches. I suppose you could make him an apple pie, too," Esther said, tilting her head. "It may convince him you could start your own business."

"You don't think he'll suspect we're up to something, do you?"

"Oh, he'll suspect something. He's always been suspicious, even as a boy. This time he'll be right, but once he tastes your apple pie, he'll be sold."

"And if he's not?"

"Then I'll introduce you to some friends at the grocer. I'm sure they'd welcome your goods."

Excitement made April feel giddy. "You think so?"

"*Jah*, they're always looking for local goods. I know apple pie isn't unique, but if I recall, your apple pie is slightly different."

April smiled to herself. She pulled out the bacon, garlic and onion to dry on a paper towel, and after removing most of the grease, she added the whipped eggs to a thin layer of the fat.

She scrambled the eggs then scooped them into a serving bowl. After she unwrapped the bread, she buttered two slices of it. "Here we go," April said as she set the bowl of eggs, the bacon and two plates on the table.

Esther closed her eyes, and April followed suit. They said their silent prayers over the morning meal, and April prayed she made it through her first day without mishap, or without upsetting Malachi.

"Amen," Esther said.

"Amen." April opened her eyes and watched as Esther slipped a bite of scrambled eggs into her mouth.

"Oh, this is *gut*. Now, tell me, what makes your apple pies so good?"

"If I told you that, it wouldn't be a secret, *jah*?"

April tried to use local honey to flavor her pies, but sometimes she explored with flavors. Occasionally, she used nutmeg instead of cinnamon. Once, she'd mixed coffee with the honey, and another time she'd added vanilla and chili powder to the cinnamon. An odd spice to put in an apple pie, but it had worked and seemed to be one of her more popular pies. "But I can make more than apple pie. I've made sticky buns and peanut butter swirl rolls. And one of my favorites is a coffee cake."

"I wonder if my nephew would be a taste tester before we hawk your wares."

April cringed. "I'm not here to catch a husband, Esther."

Esther laughed. "I know. You made that clear yesterday, and given your mourning, I think I'll quit my pressing. For now. But if you change your mind, I'll be the first to hound my nephew."

"I appreciate that, Esther," April said, even as she grew uncomfortable at the thought of being married again. She didn't think Malachi was cut from the same bolt of fabric as David. Even though he'd raised his voice last night, he'd kept his temper under control and attempted to rein in his frustration. She couldn't imagine the trouble he'd faced with Esther cutting the neighbor's roses. April believed Malachi was a *gut* man with a kind heart, but she'd thought that of David, too, and had been wrong. "I don't think I'll be changing my mind."

A soft tap sounded on the kitchen door. April and Esther turned their gazes to see who'd knocked. April's pulse sped at the sight through the glass of Malachi holding Jeb. She slid from the dining chair, smoothed her apron, and patted her bonnet. A blush warmed her cheeks when Esther's knowing smile caught her attention. April groaned, lifted her chin a little, as if she hadn't just tidied her appearance, and opened the door.

Malachi glanced at her over Jeb's shoulder and smiled. "*Gut*, you are here."

She was taken back by how handsome he looked when he smiled. The black trousers and matching vest over a light blue, long-sleeved shirt, didn't hurt none either. His black hat hung low over his brow. His rosy cheeks illuminated his blue eyes. For sure and for certain, he was a handsome man, and she'd be lying if she said she didn't find his looks appealing. "*Jah*, not sure where we'd be this time of the morning. Not many people in town stir around this time of the day, ain't so?"

Malachi laughed. "I suppose you're right," he said as he rushed in. His steps halted just inside the doorway. "What did you cook? It smells…good."

April reached out for the *boppli*. "Care to have eggs and bacon? There are plenty. Let me grab another plate."

"*Denki*," he said. "I think I have some time, but before I sit down, I have a question to ask."

April lifted an eyebrow as she unbundled Jeb. *"Jah?"*

"What did I say?" Esther mumbled.

Malachi glanced at his aunt, but April quickly drew his attention back to her. "What is your question, Malachi?"

He sighed and raked his hand over his chin. "I forgot about today's busy schedule and need someone to care for Jeb. If it's too much with Aunt Esther, I can call my client and reschedule."

"What did I say?" Esther said again.

"Of course," April said, rushing on before Malachi assumed they'd been talking about him. "It's not too much. We would love to spend the day with this little guy, wouldn't we, Esther?"

"*Jah*," the old woman said.

Biting the inside of her cheek, April silently lifted a prayer of thanks to *Gotte* for providing a way out of Esther's plans to scheme against Malachi. April didn't want any part in deceiving Malachi—or being underfoot, as Esther had called it—but she didn't think Esther would have listened to her if she'd told her no.

Malachi sat down and heaped a spoonful of eggs onto his plate. He'd eaten last night, but she'd been surprised he hadn't asked for another serving. How long had it been since he'd had a decent breakfast? When he shoved a bite of eggs into his mouth and closed his eyes, a trill of excitement curled her toes. Did he like her cooking? She waited impatiently for him to speak.

"This is good, April. Very good."

"*Denki*," April said, relieved he didn't have any complaints. She poured a cup of coffee and placed it in front of Malachi. "I can make more, if you'd like?"

"No, this is good and will sustain me until dinner."

"Will you not have lunch?" she asked. David never missed a meal, nor had her father.

"No, I don't usually have time for lunch." He shoved another bite of eggs into his mouth.

"It's not good to go so long without sustenance," April said.

"I don't always have a choice," he said around a mouthful of eggs. He gulped down his coffee. He tugged on the chain of his pocket watch that hung from a safety pin on his vest. "I'm still getting used to Jeb's demands, and this is the busy time of year for work. My time to make or grab something is limited."

"I could make something for you," April said. "It will take no time."

"Acting like a wife already," Esther said.

April narrowed her gaze. "I thought you said you would give up matchmaking?"

"I did," Esther said. "Only speaking my thoughts aloud."

"Well, mind your thoughts please," April said, trying to keep her tone easy and light. She didn't want to sound mean, but she was done with the topic of marriage. "And keep your thoughts to yourself, before Malachi has to find another companion for you."

A deep rumble of laughter filled the open area, warming April's heart. "I see I made a wise choice in offering April a job, don't you think, Aunt Esther? She won't allow you to run all over her, like you do me."

"I don't run all over you," Esther said. "If I did, you both would be married and not pretending like you don't suit each other."

"Esther!" April snapped. "Will you allow me to mourn your other nephew in peace, please?" At Esther's crestfallen look, April walked around the table and touched her shoulder. "I am sorry for my sharpness, but I don't know how many times I can say I'm not looking for a husband." April sighed and looked toward Malachi for help.

"Aunt Esther," he said. "April is correct. We thank you for caring for our well-being, but as April has said, she is mourning her husband, and you know why I won't take a wife."

This piqued April's curiosity, but she wouldn't ask why Malachi wouldn't take a wife. She supposed he'd been rejected, hurt by someone he'd once deeply cared for. She'd known someone in Haven, a young woman, who'd declared to never marry because the man she loved had married another. A valid reason as much as April's, both revolving around fear.

Deuteronomy 31:6 pierced her thoughts. *Be strong and of good courage, do not fear nor be afraid of them; for the Lord your God, He is the One who goes with you. He will not leave you nor forsake you.* She'd been afraid. Afraid for a long time. She'd feared waking up every morning as a wife to David, not knowing what sort of trouble would meet her, usually not of her doing. His death had not dissipated her fear, only perpetuated it with more of the unknown. It'd only been at the prospect of making a life for herself that fear began to fade into the shadows, but now…

Every time Esther said the words *wife* or *marriage*, that fear clawed at her chest, threatening to suffocate April. How could she move beyond fear and trust *Gotte* would go before her and not forsake her, or that He hadn't already forsaken her? She did not wish Esther to fear the unknown. April wanted her to feel secure that

Malachi and she would do all in their power to keep her safe and loved.

"I am sorry for my harsh tone and for fueling a conversation that is not my concern, Esther. I will not abandon you, but I do ask you quit speaking of marriage."

"Apology accepted, but only if you accept mine for causing you stress." Esther's shoulders shook, and she reached up to wipe her eyes with her knobby, wrinkled knuckles. She smiled up at April, but when she shifted her gaze to Malachi, the corners of her eyes crinkled in displeasure. "You shouldn't allow the past to dictate your future, Malachi. You deserve happiness, and not your parents' troubles."

April dragged in a breath, surprised Malachi's reluctance to marry had nothing to do with rejection or a broken heart, but rather from what he'd witnessed as a child, if Esther's words were any indication.

Malachi leaned back in his chair and crossed his arms. "And what makes you think I am not happy? No," he said, shaking his head. "Do not answer that. I have work. I have a home. I have you, and I have Jeb. What more do I need?"

"A helpmate."

Malachi wasn't sure how the conversation had driven back to the topic of marriage, but given the last several months of Esther hounding him to take a wife, he shouldn't have been surprised. However, he was done with the topic, and since April had shut it down as best she could given Esther's tenacity, he changed the course of the conversation. "I would appreciate a sandwich, if you don't mind?"

He shouldn't have turned the conversation back to April preparing a meal for him and granting Aunt Esther more fuel for her obsession, but he figured it was better than continuing with an argument that would further frustrate him and a pregnant woman. Besides, he'd spent weeks forgoing three meals a day, and he knew the importance of eating to maintain his energy if he were going to keep up his current pace and maintain a successful business.

"Of course, I'll throw something together quickly," April said. She held her finger to her mouth to hush Aunt Esther. Thankfully, his aunt clamped her thin lips together.

Malachi pushed from the table and stood. "*Denki*, I would like that. And *denki* for keeping Jeb," he said as he relieved her of the baby and sat back down. "I will find permanent arrangements for him today."

"Why go through the trouble?" Esther asked. "You say you're short on time. We're convenient. Right next door, *jah*? April doesn't mind."

The convenience appealed to him. However, he didn't want to take advantage of her. "What say you, April?"

She glanced up from the two sandwiches she wrapped in paper towels. Her brow furrowed, as if she hadn't heard him.

"If you're agreeable, I would pay what I would for a nanny."

"And since your room is covered for being my companion," Esther said, "you could save up to rent one of the other storefronts in town. I'm sure there are several available."

Malachi's stomach knotted. He wasn't sure he liked that idea. He didn't like to think badly of anyone, but one could never be too careful, and he didn't want April to be taken advantage of by an unscrupulous business owner. Not while she was his responsibility.

Her green eyes lit with excitement as she looked at Esther. "You think that is possible?"

"Sure, I mentioned it last night as a possibility," Esther said. "And now, with what Malachi will pay you for me and Jeb, and saving money with rent, you'll have your own store in no time. If you like, we can take little Jeb for a walk and look around town. Maybe we'll find something."

"Now, wait a minute, Aunt Esther." He laid Jeb in the crook of his elbow. "Do you think that's a good idea?"

"Of course. Jeb likes our walks."

Malachi massaged the back of neck with his free hand as he contemplated his aunt's response. He wasn't worried about them taking Jeb for a walk. His concern lay in the fact that Aunt Esther suggested April rent from an *Englischer*, as there were very few storefronts owned by members of their community that were not already in use. If he needed further proof his aunt's mind was slipping, suggesting April rent from an *Englischer* was it, especially since she trusted few of them beyond simple business dealings. She often voiced her opinion about how she felt many of his patrons took advantage of him by paying him with useless items. Like the carousel horse. Malachi had agreed he had no idea what he would do with the item, but it had some value.

"I won't lose them," April said as she took Jeb from Malachi.

He scrubbed his palm over his smooth jaw, a reminder that he was not married. And he intended to keep it that way, no matter how perfect a helpmate April would make him. In the few hours he'd become reacquainted with her, he'd found she wasn't only beautiful with her brilliant green eyes, but her strength and courage were highly admirable. As was her kindness to his family. She would make a *wunderbar fraa*, just not to him. "You misunderstand my concern." He moistened his lips and tried to think of a good way to speak his mind without offending her. "I wouldn't feel comfortable allowing you..."

April arched an eyebrow as she adjusted Jeb on her shoulder. That obviously wasn't the correct word.

"Not exactly what I meant." He groaned. "It isn't common practice around here, but there are some individuals who would seek to take advantage of a single woman they perceive as gullible." He quickly held his hand up in defense. "Not that I believe you are gullible, but others may, just by your gender alone."

"Another reason for why I should have a husband, *jah*?" April asked, irritation coloring her tone.

"I didn't say it," Aunt Esther said.

Malachi removed his hat and speared his fingers through his hair as he released a sigh. He was bungling the conversation horribly. "That's not what I'm saying.

It would be better if you were just content with caring for Esther and Jeb."

"And forget about my aspirations of owning my own store?"

"No," he said, shaking his head. "Yes. I can't see how you can manage a business, Aunt Esther, Jeb and the *boppli* when it comes along."

April stalked toward him. Her pink-tinged cheeks turned crimson, and her nostrils flared. "I am a woman. An Amish woman. I come from a long line of strong Amish women who have managed children, households and businesses, all while managing their husbands. I have been through the muck and mire and come to you now bearing the scars of tragedy and grief." She held up her free hand, scars from the fire still healing. "I can manage a business, Esther, and our *bopplis*. If you doubt me, then prove me wrong, but don't doubt me without giving me a chance. Rent the space to me. I'll show you what a woman like me can do. I won't fail."

That's what he feared, and then he'd be stuck with her. Unless, of course, he took on Aunt Esther's matchmaking scheme and found April a *gut* Amish husband.

"Renting the space to April would solve your problem, Malachi," Aunt Esther said.

He sighed; it would also add another to his shoulders. The memories stored in that space would ambush him, and there was also the matter of always being in April's presence as he helped fix the place up so it was usable.

"You can't claim I can't manage, without proof of my inability," April argued. "At least give me that opportunity. Three months. If I can't make it work by the time I have my baby, I'll concede."

Swallowing down the knot forming in his throat, he said, "And if you do succeed, what will be the ask?"

"That I continue running my own business from the space until I choose not to."

That meant for as long as he breathed, if her stubborn tenacity was any indication. She needed a husband, and quickly. He began a mental list, and just as swiftly as names popped into his head, he scratched them off the list. He'd find time later. Maybe he'd even ask Bishop Mueller for his assistance in the matter, but that might lead to a line of questioning from the bishop that Malachi wasn't ready to answer. Malachi rose from the chair, disbelieving what he was about to do. He held out his hand to her, and she eyed it with suspicion, before shaking it.

"Fair enough." He kissed the top of Jeb's head before grabbing the sandwiches April had made for him and walking out the door. "Give me a few days to clear the space."

Chapter Six

By the time the weekend came around, April began to wonder exactly what Malachi meant by a few days. Granted, he'd been busy, dropping Jeb off each morning before the sun rose and picking him up every night in time for dinner. Esther's Wednesday family dinner had turned into a nightly thing these past few nights. Every morning April had breakfast ready in case Malachi hadn't eaten before dropping his *boppli* off for the day, and she prepared lunch for him. It was the least she could do in exchange for his help in seeing her goal come to fruition.

Except it wasn't.

She adjusted Jeb onto her hip and blinked back frustrated tears. Esther pushed the empty stroller into the dark, crowded room. Nothing had changed. The carousel horse hadn't moved. Boxes were in the same position as the day she'd arrived in Garnett.

"Ah, I see he has lost track of time."

April sniffed. "Do you believe that, Esther? Or was Malachi only placating me for a time, hoping to distract me with a promise while hoping I'd be too exhausted with you and Jeb to push the matter?"

Esther picked at a scab on her hand until it began to bleed. A common occurrence these last few days. April laid Jeb into the stroller and fished a tissue from her purse. She dabbed the tissue against Esther's papery skin until the bleeding slowed.

"I did it again, didn't I?" Esther asked. "As if you don't have enough to do without cleaning me up."

April searched around in her purse for a BandAid and covered the open sore. "We'll need to go to the store and get more bandages if you continue to scratch your skin."

The older woman looked crestfallen. "I'm sorry."

"No need, Esther. Your skin has thinned with age, and it easily scratches. We just need to take care that your sores don't become festered." She released Esther's hand. "Now, what am I going to do about this?"

"We'll do it ourselves," Esther said. "We can't let all your plans go to waste. As busy as my nephew is, he'll hardly notice."

Crossing her arms, April turned, reacquainting herself with the space. The excitement she'd experienced earlier in the week as she'd mapped out her plans for the store with Esther's help, was replaced with worry. "I wouldn't feel right about going through items not my own."

"Psh," Esther said, waving her hand as she glanced around the store area. "Malachi is a man of his word. He made a business bargain with you, and he'll keep it. Don't fret. Now, where did I put the quilts I was working on for the spring market?"

April creased her brow, recalling they'd packed some

quilts away in a chest when they'd cleaned out the room she occupied at Esther's house. It was mid-August, and spring was many months away. Was Esther having another slip of the mind? She didn't want to startle her by telling her she was confused, but she wanted to bring Esther back to the present if her mind had wandered to another place and time. "Which quilts are those, Esther?"

Esther halted her perusal of the area and stared at April for a moment. April didn't move, hoping recognition would don before she made an awkward moment even more difficult. Jeb cooed, drawing Esther's attention. The older woman leaned over the stroller and touched her index finger to the blanket covering the *boppli*. "What a sweet child," Esther said, glancing over her shoulder at April. "Is he yours?"

A moment of panic raced through April's limbs. She wasn't certain how to respond to Esther's confusion as it was more prominent now than it had been during the last several days. Mental decline was not unheard of among the community she'd belonged to in Haven, but April didn't have personal experience with it. How should she respond? Truth, as with all things.

"No," April said, touching Jeb's little foot. "The *boppli* is Malachi's nephew."

She hoped speaking Malachi's name would bring recognition to Esther's mind.

"Malachi," Esther said, looking even more confused. "My boys aren't old enough—" Esther pressed her thin lips together. "I remember now. This is Jared's *boppli*.

He got into some trouble during his *rumspringa*. He still hasn't returned."

April knew Jeb was Malachi's nephew and recalled Esther mentioning Malachi's brother Jared. She couldn't help wondering what sort of man would take on the responsibility of a child not his own. Of course, it was done all the time among their communities whenever a child was in need. However, Malachi was single, with no *fraa* or *kinder* of his own. Wouldn't it have made sense for another family member to take the baby? She shook her head. Witnessing Malachi interact with the baby the last few days, she knew he was a natural *daed* for the *boppli*.

"I won't say much, but it's *gut* Jared gave the baby into his brother's keeping." Esther drew the tip of her finger over the curb of Jeb's cheek and unfolded herself. The older woman's eyes were bright and clear.

April breathed a sigh of relief and made a mental note to speak to Malachi about this latest incident. Not that she expected anything to change in the current plan of care for Esther. She'd grown fond of her late husband's great-aunt, and fond of Jeb, too. And despite that Malachi had yet to fully hold to his end of the bargain, she'd seen bits of his character over the last few days and thought him to be a *gut* Amish man, one who could be a good husband. It didn't hurt that he complimented her cooking, even the hamburger and potato dish that could have used a little more salt and pepper. Any woman would be blessed to call Malachi Stoltzfus *mann*.

"I think we should wait for Malachi before tackling this mess," April said.

"We could," Esther agreed. "That may be a while. His business causes his good intentions to be pushed aside and forgotten."

April considered Esther's words. Her late husband had often said things, but she wasn't sure David's intentions had been good or if he'd only said things to achieve his own ends. David had been hardworking with his immediate obsessions, often neglecting all else. Malachi, although scattered at times, took care of his aunt's property, his nephew and a business. He also conversed with April every day, asking her how she was doing, and he seemed genuinely interested in her response.

"Do you think we could manage moving everything to one side?" Esther asked. "I'm not as frail as I look, but I'm not as strong as I used to be either."

April slowly spun around, taking in the various items housed in the room, including the large worktable. "I think we can do anything, Esther."

Except move the carousel horse. That would have to wait on Malachi, unless she encountered a young man for hire. Of course, there was the cookstove, but that wouldn't move, since it was hooked up. She'd clean it and check to see if everything was in working order before using it, though.

"We may not be able to complete it without my nephew, but we'll get a start," Esther said. "Take note, once Malachi realizes what we're doing, he'll be here."

April didn't respond. She wasn't sure she wanted Malachi's help, and if it weren't for his belongings taking up space in the place she hoped to start her business, she wouldn't accept it. She didn't want to be beholden to anyone, but more than that, she refused to be a burden, especially to a man who thought she was his responsibility. She needed to carry her weight, if not more. If only to prove to herself she could earn her own way.

The loss of David and Samantha hadn't been her doing, and she bore the scars of trying to save them. Their deaths had been *Gotte*'s will. She accepted that, but the aftermath, the loss of family and home, had left her at the mercy of a community where she'd been an outsider. And although the members had been kind, especially Milda, they'd quickly tried to marry her off again.

April drew in a shaky breath as memories of David came to mind. She had nothing against marriage, and believed a wife should submit to her husband, as was their way. But David hadn't been an easy man, and his ventures had often left them in dire straits, filling her with worry whenever they'd been confronted by frustrated *Englischers* neighboring their land, or whenever their bishop arrived to offer counsel on David's business dealings when he failed to hold his end of the deal. Sadly, David had often made himself scarce, leaving April to relay the message, only for her words to fall on deaf and irritated ears. In David's mind, she'd had no place in his matters.

She wasn't ready to be in that position again, which is why having her own source of income and a way to support herself and the *boppli* appealed to her. Even though she liked Malachi, and sensed his character was nothing like David's had been, it would take more than trust to fully believe he would be the type of *mann* who would see his *fraa* as a true helpmate. One whose opinions were sought after and considered.

April would set out to carry more than her share of the weight while she was employed by Malachi, and she wouldn't ask him for help in making the storefront a suitable business space, other than to remove his belongings.

"Daylight is burning," Esther said, pulling April from her thoughts. "Where would you like to begin?"

April didn't have to think twice as she pointed toward the area looking out to where she hoped to make a small garden. "The alcove. It'll be a nice space for you and Jeb to relax during the day."

Esther emitted a cackle. "Always thinking about the comfort of others."

A smile curved April's mouth. "I can't say my motives are completely unselfish. However, it is the smallest, and once it is put to rights, we'll have a sense of accomplishment. And then..." She turned to the rest of the store, including the thick layers of dust coating the baseboards and the cobwebs draping the corners. She chewed the inside of her cheek, wondering if Jeb should even be in the room when she cleaned. If they timed it right, maybe Jeb and Esther would be ready for a nap. A rocker and a bassinet remained in the joining business space, and she was sure since Esther had had free roam a week ago, Malachi wouldn't mind if they invaded his office while she dusted in here. At least Esther and Jeb would be farther away from the dust.

"…we can tackle the rest. First, let's open the windows and doors to air the room out."

The moment she touched a box to move it against the dedicated wall for all Malachi's belongings, Jeb wailed. Esther and April laughed at the same time. "Well," April said, "I guess our plans will have to wait until the boss has been fed."

"I'll feed him, if you'd like," Esther said.

April liked the plan. It would give the elderly aunt something to do without April worrying about Esther getting hurt moving boxes around the room. "Of course. I'll grab a chair from Malachi's office."

The moment she opened the adjoining doors, she noticed a young man rifling through items on Malachi's desk. April gasped. The man, gaunt in the cheeks and with blond hair spiked at odd angles poking from beneath a black stocking cap, turned. Eyes nearly black pierced her. He scanned her from head to toe, landing back on her face. A red-and-black flannel covered a white shirt, and she was sure she spotted a pair of suspenders peeking from the edges of the loose buttons.

His Adam's apple bobbed.

"May I help you?" she asked.

The man's mouth moved, but no sound came out. He raced across to the door and nearly tripped down the stairs as he rushed out the front. April waited a few moments to see if the man was going to return then shut the door and locked it. It wasn't until she looked out the front window, following the man with her gaze that she noticed he wore a pair of dark trousers, not *Englisher* pants, but Amish.

She perused Malachi's office then stopped when she realized she wouldn't know if something was missing. This was another thing she'd have to speak about to Malachi. She wiped her palms down the front of her apron and snagged one of the spindle-backed chairs from the table Malachi used for his customers.

Opening the French doors, she stepped across the threshold and found Esther pointing to the side door, her hand shaking.

"Are you well, Esther?" April said as she set the chair on its four legs.

Esther turned, her wrinkling forehead furrowed in confusion. Her brow smoothed and she smiled. "*Jah*. I must have had another moment. I thought I saw someone, but I didn't."

A sigh of relief escaped April. She was pleased Esther recognized she was having slips of the mind. For a moment, April had feared the stranger had come over here and frightened Esther. Thank goodness that hadn't been the case. "I know it's uncomfortable, but we'll do our best to weather through your moments, as long as you do your best to help me weather this mess."

April winked then led Esther to the chair before grabbing Jeb from the stroller and settling him into the crook of her arm. The *boppli* gazed up at Esther and smiled. "He likes you."

"I like him, too," Esther said. "He'll be a *gut* boy. Malachi will see to that. He thinks he failed, you know."

"Who?" April asked.

"Malachi. He thinks he failed his brother, but he didn't. I was too soft on Jared after his mother died. I should have taken a sterner hand and sought help when I noticed he was acting up instead of turning a blind eye."

Esther moistened her lips, and April gripped her hand.

"I feared if I pushed..." Esther lifted her free hand to wipe the corner of her eye. Tears filled the spaces between the rigid veins raising the delicate skin. "... Jared would be like his *daed*, or worse, his *mamm*."

April wanted to close her ears to Malachi's childhood. She didn't need any more reasons to be drawn to him, especially when she refused to marry, but she couldn't unhear the words Esther had uttered during her emotional breakdown. If Esther had feared disciplining Malachi and his brother would turn them into their father, their upbringing must not have been good. To say they'd be like their *mamm* was worse. April couldn't help the ache building in her heart for a childhood Malachi hadn't had. For all his kindness in offering her a job caring for his aunt and his nephew, as well as a place to build her dreams, was there something she could do to mend some of his brokenness in return? Without opening her heart to him?

"You're d-d-doing it again."

Malachi swung the hammer against the nail then removed the three nails pinched between his lips. "What am I doing?"

"G-g-grunting." Levi Dienner stammered over his words.

The stutter caught Malachi off guard since his cousin typically only stumbled over his sounds when he was nervous. Malachi glanced around to see if anyone approached them, but since his client was out of town, and the tiny house they were building was on the man's back forty on a hundred acres about five miles outside of town, Malachi was sure he would have heard an *Englischer*'s vehicle.

"You sound like an old man stretching out of bed," Levi said, then looked down. His forearms pressed against the ridgeboard. "I haven't done anything wrong, have I?"

Malachi adjusted his hat and wiped the beads of sweat from his brow. He'd hoped for an early fall this year, but summer had northeast Kansas in its clutches, and there was no sign of the blistering heat letting go anytime soon. He tucked his hammer into his tool belt and leaned his elbows against the top ladder rung. He peered out over the pitch of the roof they were building, and beyond Levi's shoulder. Swaths of gold fell as a farmhand cut hay in the field. A line of trees bordering the back field stood proud, like ancient centuries guarding the castle gates. Their leaves glittered with various shades of yellow and red. This time last year, when he'd built a workshop for his client, he'd been nothing more than a working man who visited Aunt Esther's house weekly for dinner and to cut her lawn and do any other odds and ends she'd needed done.

He clenched his jaw. Now, her mind wasn't the same. She needed more care than he knew how to give. He worried about her. He worried about Jeb. And the pretty caregiver who would soon have her own *boppli*. Her insistence on starting her own business in the property that held too much junk caused even more memories to crash against him forcing a sense of desperation, like lightning striking a tree during the peak of a storm.

"It is not you, Levi," he said, catching his cousin's eye so he knew he meant the words as truth. "You are doing wonders, and I'm appreciative of the help. Soon, you'll be building houses on your own."

"I have a *gut* teacher." Levi smiled.

"*Jah*, you think so?" Malachi took his hammer from his tool belt and positioned a nail into the hole in the bracket. "You're a quick learner. I find it difficult to believe you never swung a hammer before a few weeks ago."

Malachi arced his hammer and brought it down against the nailhead again and again until the nail pushed against the bracket and sank into the wood.

Levi laughed.

"What do you find so funny?" Malachi tapped another nail into the next hole.

"You are avoiding my concern."

Malachi grunted. "That is not my intention. I would rather avoid the cause of my grunts, as you call them, altogether."

"It's not Jeb, is it?"

Malachi shook his head. "Esther."

"That bad," Levi asked as he slid the end of a rafter into a bracket. "Guess I should be grateful it's not me."

"She's bent on finding me a wife."

"Then I'm very grateful that it's not me," Levi said. "Our aunt can be single-minded. Is she pushing the list she gave you?"

"No." Malachi scooped another handful of nails out of the box.

"None to your liking, I suppose." Levi climbed onto the ridgeboard and crawled down the length like a cat to settle another rafter in place.

"If I was of the mind to have a wife, they may be, but you know as well as any, why I won't marry."

As kids, Malachi and Jared had been close with Abe and Levi. Although Malachi suspected not all had been right in Abe and Levi's home, they knew the troubles Malachi and Jared had suffered. Their *daed* hadn't used his fists like Levi's stepfather had. Malachi and Jared's father had been neglectful and hurtful with his words. His father hadn't honored their mother with kindness or even faithfulness. Malachi wouldn't taint a *gut* Amish woman with his father's sins. And Malachi feared he would follow his mother's path of depression, if any woman he might take for a wife held misgivings or doubted his loyalty and faithfulness.

"Seems to me, my brother felt the same," Levi said. "And now look at him. He lays about and watches clouds with Naomi, and he does it willingly."

"I can't explain what has gotten into Abe, but you don't have to worry about me catching his ailment. Not even when our great-aunt moves a woman into her house with the intentions of marrying me off."

Levi leaned back on his heels, his feet dangling off the edge of the roof. "She didn't."

"She did," Malachi said while silently praying for Levi's safety. "Our cousin David's widow. Will you remove the fear from my veins and go back to the ladder before you fall?"

His cousin's cheeks flushed a little beneath the sun and he crawled back to the ladder.

Worried he'd embarrassed his cousin, he said, "At least wait until more of the roof is set before you start acting like a squirrel jumping limb to limb. Like I said, you're a natural, but Abe would never forgive me if something happened to you."

"I'm a grown man, nearly twenty-two." Levi climbed down the ladder and moved it over a few feet before climbing back up. "He needs to quit hovering like I'm going to break. Now, tell me about this woman. Is she pretty?"

Malachi paused his work and the corners of his mouth lifted.

"She is," Levi said. "And that's the problem?"

"Not exactly," Malachi said. "I've never been tempted to marry a woman because she's pretty. In fact, I've never been tempted to marry."

Although, he had to admit to himself, if he'd been a different man, one who wasn't the son of Toby Stoltzfus, he might be tempted by April. The last few days had been nice. Coming home—well not his home, but home enough—to pick up Jeb and find a hearty meal, cooked on a stove, ready for him had given him a sense of family. At least, what he thought a real family might be.

"Esther, somehow promised April the use of my store."

"Your store?" Levi asked. "The one you're using, or the one filled with all your *mamm*'s belongings?"

Malachi half grunted, half sighed. "The latter. It needs to be cleaned, and I'm pressed for time, and then there is Jeb. I promised she could use the store to start her business in exchange for watching Jeb and Aunt Esther when I'm not around. I asked her to give me a few days, and more than a few days have passed."

"It's not like you to not keep your word, Malachi."

Malachi clenched his teeth. "Don't I know it, which is the cause for my distress."

"Then you should go," Levi said. "I can finish up the rafters, and we'll get an early start Monday morning. We'll keep on schedule."

Malachi glanced at the morning sun and the remaining brackets needing rafters. If he guessed right, it was almost nine. And, if they quit talking about April—or rather, if Malachi quit thinking about her and his responsibility to her—they could attach the plywood and underlayment then lay the metal sheeting. "We'll work until noon then call it a day. Three hours should give us time to complete the roof, *jah*?"

Levi's mouth twisted.

"Before you think I doubt your abilities, I don't," Malachi said. "I need time to prepare myself."

Laughter danced in the air. "I never thought my giant of a cousin feared anything, not even a woman."

"Heed what I am about to say, Levi." Malachi positioned the nail into the hole and swung his hammer. "There is a difference between being prepared to face an unknown situation and fear. In this case, I need to gather my mind around the work ahead of me." Work that would pepper him with memories he wasn't ready to face. "Especially considering I have work here I'd rather do."

"Since we're calling an early day, I could help, if you like," Levi said. "*Mamm* isn't expecting me until dinner."

Malachi descended the ladder, scooted it over, and climbed back up. Although Levi was family and knew Malachi's past, he wasn't sure he wanted a witness if his emotions overcame him. Then again, Levi's presence might grant him the strength and backbone he needed to get through the task ahead of him. It was something to ponder. "Let's finish the roof, and then we'll discuss the cleanup of the store."

"Sounds *gut*, boss," Levi said. "Hey, do you still have that carousel horse?"

Chapter Seven

April pressed her palms into the small of her back and stretched. The hardwood floors weren't perfect, but at least they looked clean.

"It looks *gut, jah*?" Esther asked.

Pushing to her feet, April took in all their hard work and kept her sigh in check. There was a lot yet to be done, but she wouldn't rain on Esther's sunshine. "*Jah.* We've done a lot."

"You sure have."

April jumped, her heart pounding in her chest. "Malachi, you're back early."

"I am. I came to keep my word, but it looks like you couldn't wait." He scowled. His brow furrowing with displeasure. He crossed his arms.

Out of habit, April stepped back. He twitched his mouth as he relaxed his shoulders and dropped his arms to his sides. His expression softened. She took a breath and tried to relax while pulling her shoulders back and lifting her chin to face this giant of a man. Somehow, his change in stance granted her courage and gave her confidence not to shy away from him, as she'd often done with David. Malachi would not hurt her, not with his hands or his words.

"We thought we would help," she said.

Another man, dressed in a blue shirt and black trousers held by suspenders, hovered behind Malachi. A straw hat dangled from his fingertips. A ring from his hat formed around his head, leaving curls spiking upward. She drew in another breath, thankful it was not the same man she'd seen thumbing through the papers on Malachi's worktable.

"You should have waited," Malachi said as he looked her over, halting at her hands. She hadn't noticed until that moment how much they stung from the diluted vinegar she'd used to clean the hardwood floors and the walls. "I would have completed the task."

April folded her hands behind her. "And you would have refused our help, ain't so? When all our chores were completed, we checked on the progress." She moistened her lips and hoped he accepted what she was about to say as her good intentions and not disrespect. "You're a busy man, Malachi. My desire to have my own store was not meant to add another burden to your shoulders."

"That's right, and we did no harm," Esther said as she craned her neck to see around Malachi. "Levi, come greet your aunt with a hug. It's been a few weeks, *jah*? You should come for Wednesday-night dinners. Now that April is cooking, I can promise you *gut* food."

The younger man moved from behind Malachi and embraced Esther. "It's g-g-good to see you, Aunt Esther."

April noticed the young man's stutter and sought to put him at ease once Esther released him. She nodded to the hesitant young man. "I'm April. It's nice to meet you."

"N-n-nice to meet you, cousin."

She couldn't help the curve of her mouth upward at how he addressed her, claiming her as family and not as a stranger. It felt good to have a sense of family and community. It warmed her heart to be welcomed with a genuine smile and a friendly face.

Malachi walked around the room. His gaze followed the lines of every nook and cranny. April padded close to him, liking the feel of her bare feet against the freshly scrubbed floor. "As you can see, there are a few things we didn't move, like the old stove, the register and the horse."

He glanced at her over his shoulder. The softness and interest in his eyes spurred her to say more.

"I want to use this space here for canned goods, then baked goods here. And on the shelves over here, I'd like to fill with homemade soaps and candles. There will be a place for quilts and rugs," she said as she walked toward the alcove. Excitement vibrated through her as she envisioned what this space would become. "Over here, I want to create a little space for Jeb and my *boppli.* I thought of putting the bassinet here and bringing in a rocker. With your permission, I'd like to clean up the area outside, too. When spring comes around, I think a hummingbird feeder and a lot of bright flowers would look nice, *jah*?" She glanced up at him at his silence. "And, of course, I'd like to add some green plants inside here," she said, motioning to the windows. "It'll brighten the place and add some cheer, don't you think?"

"And how do you intend to stock your store?"

His question was fair. "Well, mostly, I'll make many of the items, but I thought to offer space to other ladies in the community to sell their goods. I think it'll be *gut* to be part of a community again." She longed for the close friendships she'd once had before her marriage to David. "And Esther tells me Garnett has a flower nursery. Butterfly Gardens. I thought about approaching them, as well, to see if they would like to sell some of their seasonal goods out front."

"You have thought this through," he said, propping his hands on his hips. "Levi will assist me in moving the bigger items out, and then we'll break for lunch."

She bit her lip as guilt tapped on her shoulder that she had been so focused on cleaning she hadn't realized the time. Esther must be hungry. Her stomach growled, and Malachi laughed. She caught his gaze and saw the teasing glint. "I see you've forgotten to feed yourself, too."

"*Jah*," she said, smiling at his handsome face. Something swirled inside her chest, feeling bubbly like a soft drink through a straw on a hot day. It was almost like the same feeling she'd had as a child when she and her siblings ran through the soft grasses during spring. And she could only attribute that to joy—something she hadn't felt for several years—and this… This… whatever *this* was, had never been a result of David's laughter or actions. In fact, she couldn't recall ever feeling this sort of joy during her marriage. Not once. "I…

I should take Esther and Jeb to the house. I'll prepare us some lunch."

"And afterward, we'll discuss more of your plans."

She dipped her head. *"Denki."*

April picked Jeb up from the stroller. "Let's go make some lunch, Esther."

They walked out the back door, across the alleyway and through Esther's backyard. The sensation of hard wood, cement, gravel and grass in a matter of a few moments brought to mind *Gotte*'s word. The parable of the sower, from Luke, chapter eight.

A sower went out to sow his seed: and as he sowed, some fell by the way side; and it was trodden down, and the fowls of the air devoured it. And some fell upon a rock; and as soon as it was sprung up, it withered away, because it lacked moisture. And some fell among thorns; and the thorns sprang up with it, and choked it. And other fell on good ground, and sprang up, and bare fruit an hundredfold.

She knew *Gotte* was speaking about *Gotte*'s word, but she couldn't help see how David's leadership of their household had been much like sowing on rocky ground—or rather, he was the rocky ground and she was the sower. Her love had done little to appease him or to bring him joy. Her efforts at submitting to him were often rebuffed and criticized. But in the moments she'd shared with Malachi, it seemed as if he was the sower and she was the ground. The more kindness and consideration he showed her, the more she thirsted for time with him.

They approached the back steps to Esther's home

and April lifted her face to the warm midday sun. Like a flower opened to the bright goodness offered by the sun, she felt as if she were blooming. Thriving. And she hungered and thirsted for more of Malachi's goodness. For the first time since the death of her late husband, she recognized the possibility that she and Malachi could make a good partnership. Not just as business partners, but as *mann* and *fraa*.

She opened the door, and assisted Esther up the stairs before following her into the kitchen. She laid Jeb in his bassinet and washed her hands. "I'm sorry for the late lunch. You must be hungry."

"I'm a grown woman, April," Esther said. "If I wanted to interrupt our chores and eat, I would have said as much."

A chair scraped across the floor and April turned around just as Esther sat. "Still, I'm sorry. I should have paid closer attention to the time."

"If you bring me the bread, I'll make slices while you throw a salad together," Esther said.

"Sure," April said as she set a towel-wrapped loaf in front of the elderly woman along with a plate and a knife. "I'll heat some leftovers, too."

They had some meat-and-potato casserole remaining from the night before, the meal that Malachi had enjoyed. April stirred the embers within the stove then turned up the heat. She pulled the leftovers and the makings for the salad from the refrigerator. Her hands moved quickly as she chopped lettuce, tomatoes, carrots and onions into a large salad bowl then seasoned it with pepper before drizzling vinegar oil on top to enhance the natural flavors of the vegetables.

"I know you were saving the apple pie you made this morning for dinner, but I think lunch will be good," Esther said. "That way, nephew Levi can get a taste, too. Oh, and you should send the extra one home with him to give to his sister-in-law, Naomi. She and Abe recently had their own *boppli*. My memory fails me, but he's not much older than Jeb. I believe. It would be *gut* to share your pies, and the kindness will gain you a friend, too, *jah*?"

A friend? April hadn't had many since she'd left home. Only one when she'd lived in Haven with David, but he hadn't taken kindly to her visiting, and even less kindly to her having visitors. Eventually, she'd quit trying to plan visits with her friend, as it saved a lot of boisterous arguments. "A friend would be nice, especially one who is a mother. Would Malachi approve?" The surprise on Esther's face took April back. Had she said something wrong? "I mean since Naomi is his cousin's wife, I wouldn't want Malachi thinking I'm..." She couldn't find the right word she wanted to say.

"Trying to manipulate him into marriage?"

"Not exactly. Well, yes."

"Is that what you're doing by making him breakfast, lunch and dinner? He doesn't pay you for his meals, only for keeping me company and watching Jeb."

"No," April said, shaking her head. "I have no interest in being married again. I only want to thank him for the opportunities he's given me, but I don't wish for

Malachi to mistrust my intentions if I sought a friendship with his cousin's wife."

Esther lifted herself from the chair and shuffled across the kitchen floor. She laid her hand on April's arm. "I loved nephew David, just as I love all my nieces and nephews, but I know he wasn't easy. He was a hard man. I witnessed how he treated others with my own eyes. That doesn't mean Malachi is the same, as I'm sure you've witnessed in the short time you've known him. He's a *gut* man."

April swallowed the hard knot forming in her throat. She wouldn't confirm Esther's suspicions about her marriage to David, as she supposed her late husband had been a good man in his own way, and it was one thing to think about a thing and quite another to voice it aloud. David had been a hard man, which is something she would have known had she taken the time for courting, instead of rushing out of her *daed*'s home to make room for his new *fraa* and her *kinder* when they hadn't asked her or expected her to. She had to keep reminding herself, marrying David had been her choice. She'd reaped what she'd sowed by not taking the time to court her future husband. She wouldn't make that mistake again.

Esther squeezed her arm. "I think you're coming to like Malachi."

Had Esther paid attention to the interaction between her and Malachi at the store? Had she seen how April reacted to Malachi's teasing? Had she seen April smile and heard her laughter? April hoped not. She didn't need encouragement where her feelings with Malachi were concerned. What stirred in her chest earlier wasn't love, but attraction. An attraction to more than his handsomeness. His kindness drew her like a hummingbird to sweet nectar, and that was more dangerous to her resolve to remain unmarried than if she just found him handsome, but she wasn't about to say as much to Esther. "Malachi may be a *gut* man, but I am not looking for a husband, and Malachi has made it clear he is not looking for a *fraa*."

"All I'm saying, dear child, is don't let the past dictate your future. If fear is keeping you from looking for a husband, you should seek *Gotte*'s will in the matter. If wisdom is keeping you from wanting to marry again, then be wise enough to know circumstances change." Esther's eyes took on a faraway look, and April wondered if Esther was about to slip away from the present. "Take it from an old woman who has years of decisions behind her, both good and bad. Don't forsake the goodness in front of you due to stubborn pride, or you may find yourself childless and alone."

April touched Esther's hand where it lay against her forearm and took in a shaky breath. What stories did Esther have capsuled in her mind? "Esther, you are not alone. You have Malachi and Jeb. And it seems you have Abe and his family and Levi. And if they all fail you, which they won't, you will always have me."

Esther pulled back and cackled. "That is sweet of you, April, but my nephews will all have families of their own before I take my last breath. I hope to see them married before I lose too much more of myself. And you will have Jeb and your *boppli*."

"You are family, Esther," April said. "It may be through marriage to my late husband, but that doesn't change things. I will stay by your side."

"Like Naomi, Ruth and Boaz. If only Malachi was a willing kinsman redeemer."

"You forget, I would have to be a willing Ruth, too." The *boppli* stretched against her stomach and she rubbed her belly.

"Soon, you will have your hands full enough with Jeb and your baby, what would you do with an old woman like me?"

Affection for Esther filled her chest, the warmth of joy filled her cheeks. "I would love and care for her as if she was my own mother."

Malachi hadn't meant to eavesdrop, but he couldn't help hearing April's words as he climbed the porch steps. A sense of pride at April's willingness to take on Aunt Esther and love her as her own told him he hadn't been wrong in asking April for her help. However, he couldn't help sensing he needed to be cautious. He wouldn't change his mind about marriage. He couldn't afford to. Neither could she, if she wanted to establish herself within the community. And marriage was exactly where his thoughts had been leading in the moments between laying his head down and finding his sleep. It wasn't because he felt a responsibility toward her, but, for once in his life, he was beginning to understand what *Gotte*'s word meant when it said it was not good for man to be alone, and why He'd created a helpmate for Adam.

April was a *wunderbar* helpmate. Or she would be, if he would allow it, but he couldn't. The moment she discovered his parents' past—of his father's infidelity and drinking, of his mother's depression—she wouldn't be able to look at him without suspicion, and wonder if he was just like his family.

Malachi laid his phone on top of the windowsill just outside Aunt Esther's kitchen door.

"I'm starved," he said as he stepped over the threshold. "I hope you are, too, Levi." He swept his hat from his head and tapped it against his leg before hanging it on the hat tree. April shifted her attention from Aunt Esther to him. Her beautiful green eyes glittered with affection. Part of him wished that fondness was for him, but having heard what she'd told Aunt Esther, he knew the affection was not.

She led his aunt to the table. "We made salad and leftovers."

"And pie," Aunt Esther said, making Malachi's taste-buds water. Every night April had made dessert and sent a piece in his lunch the following day. She'd gone above and beyond in her kindness to him.

"It all sounds *gut*." He motioned to Levi to follow him to the sink and turned on the water. "You're in for a treat. I didn't think anyone could bake better than your sister-in-law Naomi, but April surpasses her."

"I won't be the one to tell my sister-in-law that," Levi teased. "Even if it's true."

He dried his hands on a dishtowel and held out a chair and motioned for April to sit. "You've done enough. Let me set the table."

She blinked at him in shock. He smiled and nodded toward the chair. *"Denki."*

Malachi laid out the plates then added the salad bowl and the potato-and-meat casserole. He took his chair next to April and bowed his head. He silently prayed, thanking *Gotte* for sending April to them, even if it was due to his aunt's misguided intentions. He thanked *Gotte* for the food and the hands who made it. His prayer lost focus. He opened his eyes and looked around the table. Aunt Esther, Levi and April were silently praying, the latter with her hands folded in her lap and bright red curls springing from her cap. She was pretty. Her heart-shaped face, full lips and almond-shaped eyes were so ingrained in his mind that he saw her when he closed his eyes to sleep. Even when he'd closed them to pray, he'd seen her, which wasn't good. He rubbed his hands down his thighs and pulled in a breath. April lifted her head and caught him staring. A twinge of an ache murmured in his chest. It built to a hard thump until his heart pounded in his ear. He cleared his throat. "Amen."

A chorus followed the single word. Utensils clinked against the bowls as Aunt Esther and Levi dug into the salad and the casserole.

Levi shoveled a spoonful of casserole into his mouth. "Mmm, this is good."

"*Denki*," she said.

"You should taste the salad, too." April pushed lettuce around on her plate with her fork. "The vegetables were picked fresh from the garden this morning."

Had he made her uncomfortable? He would have

to watch his actions closer and keep his distance. He didn't want to give her the wrong idea, just in case she changed her mind about marriage. "It's good, April. *Denki* for lunch."

"Of course," she said without looking up at him.

"Are you going to church tomorrow?" he asked before he thought better of it.

April finally looked at him. His pulse sped, and even though he wasn't pleased with his reaction to her simple response, ease unlocked the tension in his shoulders. He smiled at her.

"If I had directions, I suppose I could manage, if Esther would like to go."

"It's at the Chupps' home," Aunt Esther said. Her forehead creased. Malachi's heart sank as confusion made itself clear on his aunt's brow. "Or maybe that was last service."

"No, you're right, Esther," Levi confirmed. "But it's not until next week. Naomi reminded me when she was in a fester yesterday. Her loaves of bread had burned, and when I commented on how we'd love to have crispy bread to go with our meal after church, she threatened to send me visiting to Judith's home with a loaf. Judith is not on my list of girls to court." Levi's cheeks turned bright red. "I could pick you and April up next week." Levi looked at Malachi. "If you don't mind, cousin?"

A bit of jealousy poked him like a cocklebur in his bare foot. He didn't want to admit that Levi's offer had spurred the emotion, but there was no other cause for it. Why did he care if Levi escorted April and Aunt Esther to church? Because they were his responsibility. Not his cousin's. "I can manage."

Levi sputtered and took a sip of lemonade. Aunt Esther looked at him with a considering eye. And April… well, she offered a soft sweet smile. Why was he acting like a nervous boy about to ask a girl to go for a buggy ride for the first time? Church was more than a week away.

"*Denki,*" April said. "Until I gain familiarity with the community, I would appreciate the assistance."

"You'll get a chance to meet Naomi and all the *kinder.*"

A sense of pride washed over Malachi. He couldn't wait for his cousin and Naomi to meet April. Of course, it had nothing to do with the ideas forming in his head, and everything to do with providing April with community, especially since she would soon have a *boppli* to care for. Besides, what better way could he show support of her goals than by being the one to introduce her to the community. Once they took to her—and they would because how could they not—they would offer her help in growing her business.

"I look forward to meeting everyone," she said as she stood and cleared her plate from the table.

Malachi noticed she'd hardly touched her food. Was she ill? Was watching Jeb and Aunt Esther too much of a burden on her? If so, how would she manage the store, too?

"I know it's a week away, but what should I make for dinner after the service?"

He hadn't asked her about going to church to give

her more to do, but rather to introduce her to the community. But with his asking, he hadn't intended to attend service himself. "After I finish moving the boxes from the shop to the upstairs, what if you show me how to make apple pie?"

Levi burst into laughter. Malachi narrowed his eyes until his cousin fell silent. "Don't say a word, without thought, Levi. April has gone out of her way to help with Aunt Esther and Jeb. The least I can do is peel some apples."

"Mmm-hmm," Aunt Esther mumbled around a mouthful of potatoes. "I think you have an ulterior motive, isn't that right, Levi? Besides, pie making is on Tuesdays, not Saturdays."

"*Jah*," Levi agreed.

Malachi sighed and pushed up from his chair. It didn't matter if he had an ulterior motive or not. He'd seen the bright redness of the scars on her hands and the way some of her skin was near white as paper. He'd never experienced a serious injury before but had paper cuts and knicks from smashing his thumb with a hammer on the occasion. The sting of vinegar in those open wounds when he'd helped Esther with the cleaning remained with him. He couldn't imagine April's extreme discomfort on those recent burns and healing flesh. The least he could do was help peel apples and slice them for the pie. Especially when he was the one who'd brought up going to church. "I would not know what ulterior motive that would be. Now, shall we get to moving boxes?"

Before Levi could answer, Malachi's phone rang. He turned and glared at the open window where his phone perched on the windowsill on the outside. He should have left it at the office, but since he should still be on the job site, he'd brought it with him in case one of his crewmen at another site needed him. "Excuse me."

He stepped outside, snagged his phone, and walked a few feet from the window. "Hello?" he said.

Malachi listened to the voice on the other end and tried not to worry about the mishap. His friend, Uri, had cut his hand and needed medical attention. "*Jah*, Seth. Don't worry about gathering up the tools. Tell Mr. Bassett, it'll be about an hour before I make it there. You get Uri's hand wrapped and make your way to the hospital."

He ended the call and placed it on the ledge of the window before heading back inside. Malachi ducked inside.

"My apologies. Levi, there's been an accident at the Bassett site. We need to go." He took his hat from the hat tree and caught April's concern. Her purity and kindness, the way her eyes mirrored her heart and her emotions, lured him like bees to honey. She was an open book to him, and he wanted to reassure her all would be right. But doing so would only encourage his thoughts to continue down a road that was closed to him. The bridge to his heart was out and there was no reconstructing one, because he didn't even know how to secure the footings for such a monumental construction. He studied the hat in his hand. "April, *denki* again for the delicious lunch. I'll have to finish the cleanup later, if you don't mind?"

"Yes, of course," she said as she handed him a bag. "There are two slices of pie and some lemonade inside."

His manners forced him to look at her as he accepted the gift she offered. Her eyes were so beautiful and seeking, as if she could see into his thoughts and knew all the secrets he kept inside, even the ones he'd never spoken aloud. He wanted to touch her hands and ease the parts of her he knew had to cause her pain. He wanted to offer her comfort and erase the things that scared her and made her jump whenever he raised his voice a little or became stern. And, *Gotte* help him, he wanted to touch his mouth to her soft pink lips. Her russet lashes brushed against the curve of her cheeks, and he couldn't help wondering if she had read his thoughts just then. Did she know he wanted to hold her hand and kiss her?

"Levi, please take the pie plate to your family," she said with such tenderness that Malachi felt a pang of jealousy at not being the sole recipient of her attention.

"*Denki*," Levi said, and then laughed. "They'll be fighting over the crumbs."

Malachi dropped his hat onto his head. "*Denki*," he said as he walked out the door before he gave in to his wish. "I'll see you when I pick up Jeb later."

Chapter Eight

Malachi waited for Levi to sit in the seat before he flicked the reins. Worry about Uri and thankfulness at having an excuse not to spend more time around April before he did something stupid warred within his thoughts. He just wished Uri's injury hadn't been the excuse he'd needed to flee his cousin's widow.

"The way you rushed out of there reminded me of Abe when he didn't know what to do about Naomi," Levi said.

"You misunderstand, Levi," he said, trying not to grit his teeth at his cousin's observation. "Uri is injured. It doesn't sound good. Seth is taking him to the hospital as we speak."

"I'm sorry, Malachi." Levi shifted in his seat. "I hope it's nothing serious."

"Me, too. Once we finish up at the job site, we'll stop at the hospital and check on him, and then we'll drive out to Butterfly Gardens and see his *fraa*, Emmaline, if need be."

Levi scratched his forehead. "Emmaline, she'll be worried."

"*Jah*, she will be." Malachi clenched his jaw. The

pair were newly married and building a house near her *daed*'s nursery so she could be close enough to help run the family business. Uri was a natural farmer. He grew crops and raised goats. The man knew how to fix little odds-and-ends things around the farm, but he could be clumsy, and they often joked how Uri was a walking accident. When Uri wanted to build a home for Emmaline with his own hands, he'd asked Malachi if he could work on a crew to gain the needed experience. Malachi regretted that decision.

"Don't worry, Malachi," Levi said. "I'm sure he will be fine."

"I hope you're right," he said as he considered firing every man on his crew, including Levi. While they were on his job sites, they were his responsibility. However, that sense of responsibility never left, even after they called it a day. He knew he shouldn't, as it went against *Gotte*'s word, but he often worried about whether the men who worked for him made it home, or if he'd taught them well, not just with constructing a building with quality and care, but in matters of safety while using power tools. He shuddered at the thought of how much damage could be done to a man's bone and flesh when it tangled with a running blade.

Malachi cared too much and didn't wish for anything bad to happen to any of them, which was another reason he couldn't take a *fraa.* Jeb, Esther, April and the men who worked for him were enough. He could let the men go, work his business alone. He could pretend April was nothing more than a cousin or a sister, except that she wasn't. There was no way to trick his mind into thinking otherwise. Especially when she always found her way into his thoughts. However, he could find a *gut* Amish man for her to marry. Except, just as he disregarded every single woman within the community on the list Aunt Esther had given him, he'd done the same with every single man he'd come up with on his mental list. None of them was suitable for April, not even the man who sat beside him.

"It's times like this I wish we drove cars," Levi said, tearing Malachi from his thoughts.

"Agreed," Malachi said. "But we get along just fine. If Seth thought Uri needed a car, he would have asked Mr. Bassett to take them."

"Knowing Uri, he wouldn't have accepted it," Levi said around a mouthful of food. "He doesn't like cars and won't even use the tractor on his *daed*'s farm."

"True." Malachi looked at his cousin. "What are you eating?"

"Apple pie," Levi mumbled. "It's really *gut*. Delicious. Never had anything like it before. Whoever marries April will gain a *wunderbar* cook."

"I guess I'll find out when I eat my slice."

"Oh," Levi said. "You said I could have yours. It's all gone."

"Tell me you didn't eat the pie April sent for Naomi."

"Oh, no," Levi said. "Naomi'd hang me out to dry on the line if I did that. It's safe in the back."

"I believe you're right, and who knows what April would have done."

"She probably would have made me take that carousel horse of yours home."

Malachi burst into laughter. For the first time since they'd left Esther's home, the tension in his shoulders relaxed. "She doesn't like it much, does she?"

"I like her," Levi said right before he gulped down the lemonade April had packed. "She's not like some of the women in our community."

That took Malachi back. "What do you mean?"

"Nothing bad about all the others. Esther did give you a well-thought-out list of single women you could court."

"But?" Malachi tightened his grip on the reins, sensing his cousin was about to take Esther's side in the matter of his future. Surely his cousin, of all people, understood why he couldn't marry.

"Well, it's just..." Levi said as he sat back and tucked his thumbs into his suspenders. "She makes *gut* pie and is an excellent cook."

Malachi took his eyes off the dirt road ahead of them and glared at Levi. "And?"

"She suits you, Malachi." Levi held his palm up between them. "Before you get defensive, hear me out. She makes you smile."

"I smile," Malachi said. He pulled his mouth back and showed his teeth in a forced display of happiness. "A lot. See, I'm smiling."

"Not like that, you goose," Levi said, then cleared his throat. "You're more relaxed around her, even when you're irritated. She matches you step for step. You're both stubborn, trying to prove to the other you don't need each other."

"You saw all that in the short time you spent with her?"

"*Jah*, and she doesn't let you walk over her. She has a strength that I've only seen in Naomi. She seems to know what you need before you do and is a willing helpmate. A *gut* one, as far as I can tell."

Hadn't Malachi thought the same thing? He shook his head. "Even if I wanted a wife, she does not want a husband."

"Then convince her she does."

Malachi pressed his mouth into a firm line. He was walking down a dangerous road. "And how, wise one, do you suggest I do that?"

"You could court her."

A rumble of laughter filled his chest. "That will never happen."

Too many times, he'd seen his *daed* yell and bluster at his *mamm*, walk out, be gone for days, return with a bouquet, claiming to court his wife, and make apologies, only to hear his mother's sobs as it started all over again. Courting was nothing more than empty actions to manipulate another into believing what wasn't real.

"Then I guess you could prove to April she needs a husband."

He could, but Levi was right about one thing. April had a strength Malachi had only seen in Naomi—and that only after her parents had died and she set out to prove she could be a mother to seven orphaned *kinder* and keep them in the home they loved. However, Naomi wouldn't have been able to do that without Abe's own sacrifice. April's strength came somewhere from within her. She was determined to do everything on her own, and Malachi had a sense that was born from being married to David. Her skittish demeanor and the way she jumped when Malachi raised his voice indicated his cousin's marriage to April hadn't been good.

He'd watched from the outskirts as Abe had navigated the tumultuous waters of love, and it hadn't been good. Even though Malachi was coming to appreciate April and seek out her company, he could never love her. His caring started and stopped at being responsible for her. That was all. He'd seen enough from his own *daed* and his *bruder* Jared that the Stoltzfus men weren't capable of loving a woman the way she deserved, and sensing April had already had one difficult marriage, he wouldn't shackle her to a loveless one when she was worthy of so much more.

"What should we do the rest of the afternoon?" April asked.

"We could go back to the store," Esther said. "Seeing it taking shape brings back memories, and it feels *wunderbar* to be doing something useful."

"All right," April said. "I have an idea. What if we grab some of your scrap fabrics and take them over with us to see how the old sewing machine works?"

A gleam lit Esther's aging eyes, and April's heart warmed at her elderly friend's spark. "That sounds *wunderbar.* Can I give it the first go?"

April laughed. "Well, we'll see about that. I think I should try it first after we make sure the needle and thread are good, *jah*?"

Esther opened the door leading to the upstairs and disappeared in a rush. April couldn't imagine anything that would cause her more joy than to see Esther's enthusiasm. "I'll be up in a moment."

She stretched her back, then waddled over to check on Jeb. The *boppli* was sound asleep, his little lips suckling on air. "I'll be right back, wee one."

Leaving the door open so she could hear Jeb cry, she navigated the stairs with the pace of a turtle. Once she reached the top, she took a moment to catch her breath and waited for the tightening in her stomach to calm. According to her calculations, she wasn't due for another two and a half months, but since she hadn't seen a midwife, she had no confirmation of her time. The baby would come when its time was right, but she prayed it didn't come too early. Besides, from her understanding and attending to her own *mamm* through many childbirths, minor contractions came earlier with each pregnancy.

She followed the light to the open door at the end of the hall and found Esther digging through a plastic tote of fabrics. Various shades of blue covered the bed. "I should make Jeb a quilt for this coming winter, *jah*?"

The project was a little more than she thought Esther could handle in her current state of mind, but April wasn't going to extinguish the flame of purpose. "That would be *wunderbar*."

"And," Esther said as she tossed some browns, pale greens and light yellows beside the blue scraps of fabric, "a sunny one for your *boppli*. I think it's a girl, the way you're carrying, but you two have brought so much sunshine to this house, the colors of a sunflower will be *gut*."

Esther looked to April for approval. April smiled. "Whatever you choose will be *gut* and appreciated. I'm glad we could bring some joy to you." April rubbed her stomach as another contraction tightened. A small cry trickled up the stairs. "I'm going to check on Jeb, and then I'll come back to help you carry your findings downstairs."

"Take your time. I have another quilt in mind, I just have to find the right box," she said as she snapped the lid back into place.

"Would you like me to get another down for you?" April asked, her mind tuned to Jeb's soft cry.

"No, see to the boy," Esther said. "I'll only dig through the ones I can reach. Wouldn't want to break a hip and cause more work for you." Esther laughed at her joke.

"*Denki* for the consideration. I'll be right back."

She moved a little faster down the stairs when Jeb's cry became louder and more urgent. Something was wrong. She stopped dead in her tracks when her feet touched the living room floor. She gasped. Her scream stuck in the back of her throat.

A man, the same one who'd been in Malachi's shop earlier, bounced Jeb in his arms. He spun on his booted heels, his eyes wide. He kissed the top of Jeb's brow and gently laid him down in the bassinet.

Realization hit April and she relaxed a little. "You must be Jared."

The man turned to leave.

"No, wait," she said. Her heart pumping hard in her chest, she rushed the few steps across the room and grabbed hold of his flannel shirt. "Don't go yet."

He glared at her hand. The pulse in the side of his jaw ticked furiously. Although he was nearly as tall and wide as Malachi, his face was pale and gaunt. "I don't know what trouble has found you, but the least I can do is feed you."

He didn't say a word, but the drop of his shoulders told her he'd accept her offer. The floor above them creaked and his eyes once again went wide with panic. Jared started for the door.

"Please, wait," April said. "I'll be quick."

She grabbed an old flour sack from a drawer. She rummaged through the cabinets and found two Mason jars of meat and some soup she and Esther had made the day before. She topped it off with what was left of the butter from the counter and a fresh loaf of bread.

She was pleased to find Jared still hovering near the door, and she held the sack out to him.

"*Denki*," he said as he reached a shaky hand out to take the bag. "Your kindness won't be forgotten." The young man looked toward the bassinet and then bowed his head, but not before April saw a tear leak from the corner of his eye. He rushed out the kitchen door and headed toward the front of the house, the opposite direction of Malachi's shop.

With her heart still pounding in her chest, April picked up Jeb from the bassinet and cooed near his ear as she rocked back and forth. "I suppose you're hungry, too."

The floor above her head creaked again. "Shall we grab your bottle and go upstairs?"

As soon as she entered Esther's sewing room, she sat on a spindle-backed chair and began feeding the *bopli.* Her heart had yet to settle after the encounter with Jared. She wouldn't mention his presence to Esther and risk unsettling her when she seemed too content digging through fabrics, but she would tell Malachi the first moment she had an opportunity to.

He needed to know Jared had been here and in the shop. He needed to know she'd found Jared holding the baby, even if he became upset with her for not keeping a better eye on Jeb. Even if he became angry enough to send her on her way. Something this important wasn't something she could keep from Malachi. She didn't think Jared would hurt the child, but he might try to take the baby if he could.

If Malachi allowed her to stay, she promised to be more vigilant, but she'd had no idea anyone would just walk into Esther's home, and she never suspected the man from earlier this morning had been Malachi's wayward *bruder.*

"You have quite the collection there," April said, nodding toward another pile of fabric. "And what do you plan on making with all that?"

Esther gently touched the white pieces with so much longing and care. "This was to be my wedding quilt. I think it's about time I finish it and give it to a *wunderbar* home."

April's eyes widened. "I didn't know you were married."

"I wasn't. My dear Leonard…we courted for many months, as was proper." Esther's gaze went to another time and place, and filled with a mixture of love, happiness and sorrow. April knew those emotions all too well. She'd experienced that mixture in the days after David and Samantha's deaths. Sorrow at the loss, happiness that she'd loved such a lovely child—a child both *Gotte* and David had gifted her with. For that she could never regret her marriage to David, even if he'd not been the kindest of men.

"He'd asked me to marry him, and planned to ask my *daed* the next day, but an accident occurred while plowing," Esther said as emotion filled her voice and her eyes. "No one is certain what happened, except his neck was broken and the horse was found dragging the plow two neighbors' houses over."

April reached out and touched Esther's shoulder. "I'm sorry for your pain."

Esther's shoulders shook. "As you know, it's *Gotte*'s will."

"You never married," April said. "Or had *bopplis* of your own."

"No," Esther said in a mere whisper. "And I have no regrets, except maybe now. I had nieces and nephews to keep me content, and parents to help. Now, I wish I had *kinder* to take care of me so Malachi didn't have to bear that burden."

She glanced at Jeb in the crook of her arm. He wasn't a child of her body, but she loved him like her own, even if she'd known him for only a short time. Was that how Esther felt about her nieces and nephews?

"I didn't need to know love again when I'd known it so well." A lone tear rolled over the ridge of Esther's translucent cheek. "I didn't want to know that grief again."

April chewed on her lower lip. Esther hadn't married because of the love she'd shared with Leonard. April was hesitant to marry again because she hadn't known love. Was she stealing joy from herself and her child if she didn't marry? Was it possible to know the sort of love Esther had known? An image of Malachi's handsome face and broad shoulders came to her mind. His wide shoulders carried so much responsibility, and she knew he would make room for more responsibilities if the occasion arose. That was just the sort of man he was. But could April risk stepping into a union with a man she'd only known for a short time? She'd done that before, and she'd paid the consequences for it. Granted, David had only showed her what he'd wanted her to see. Until after their wedding.

She'd seen Malachi's frustration, anger, laughter and, most importantly, his love. He loved well and he loved big. She'd seen him lovingly hold Jeb and care for him, even though he wasn't Malachi's child. And she'd seen him lovingly care for an aunt whose mental slips caused him trouble. Malachi was a *gut* man. "You know Malachi would not have it any other way."

Even as she said the words, she knew they were the truth. She pulled the bottle from Jeb's mouth and propped him against her shoulder. Even if Malachi changed his mind about marriage, could she push beyond her fear of the unknown and marry again?

"I know. He's a gut man. Always has been, no matter what life has dealt him."

Once again Esther had dropped hints about the childhood Malachi had endured, and once again April wondered if there was something she could do to bless him, to show him he was a good, kind man. For a start, maybe she could finish cleaning the store, so he didn't have to. She wanted to ask about the trials Malachi had experienced, other than that he'd taken in his nephew, but rightness overcame her curiosity. Since the day was growing long and there was still much to do, she redirected Esther's focus.

"If you'll hold Jeb a moment, I'll pack all your pieces into a bag, and we'll walk to the store," April said as she handed the baby to Esther and then laid the pieces of folded fabric neatly into another flour sack she'd brought upstairs with her. "I'm excited to see how these will turn out. Maybe we can move that big table under the lantern and work later if we want to."

"That'll be good, but don't forget we have apples to peel and pies to bake, too," Esther said. "I'm sorry my nephew had to leave when he did."

Warmth spread throughout her limbs with a sense of pride for Malachi and the care he showed for those around him. She recalled the worry marring his brow and the haste with which he'd left. His life might be a little chaotic, and too busy by far, but as far as she could tell, that spoke volumes about his character. His friends, family and clients mattered to him. He hadn't said what sort of accident had happened, but given Malachi's demeanor, she could only guess that it was bad. "He cares deeply for others. He may not say as much, but he wears his heart on his sleeve, and I think he gets that from you, Esther. You did well raising him and his *bruder*."

When Esther's brow furrowed, April said, "If Malachi's character is any indication, I'm sure Jared has a *gut* heart, too. It just may take a little time to appear."

Esther's thin lips pressed together. She rubbed her finger over Jeb's little cheek, and April could only imagine the older woman's thoughts. If April were in Esther's position, she'd want the best for all her family, even Jared.

"Well, it was obvious Malachi was worried," April said. "And I'm sure, given the same situation, Jared would have been, too. Do you think there is anything we can do for whoever was hurt in the accident?"

"Not until we hear something," Esther said. "There is no way of knowing who may have been hurt or how bad the accident might have been. If it were bad enough, we will hear soon."

"That's true. I just hope no one was hurt badly."

Even as she said the words, gratitude filled her that Malachi wasn't the one who'd been injured. But she still felt for him. She carried his worry for his friend, even though she had no right or responsibility to. She wasn't Malachi's wife, and having known each other no more than a week, they were barely acquaintances. Still, she couldn't help the desire to offer him support and a listening ear when he came home. If she asked how he was when he came to pick up Jeb, would he tell her, or would he brush her off as if she wasn't worth his words or his time?

Chapter Nine

It was dark by the time Malachi returned to his aunt's. For some reason he wasn't surprised to find light filtering through the windows of the storefront he'd promised April she could use. She was stubborn and determined, of that he was certain.

He pulled his buggy to the back and climbed out. Looking up at the night sky, gratitude for the stars shining bright filled him. He looped Chaucer to the hitching post in case he decided it was time to go home whether or not Malachi was ready. Chaucer snuffed noisily. "I know, boy. It's been a long day for me, too, but longer for you, *jah*?" Malachi said as he scratched Chaucer's nose. "I'll see if I can steal you some apples before we go home."

Chaucer knickered and bobbed his head. Malachi gave him one last rub before filling the feed bag attached to the hitching post with oats. With all the work Malachi had had lately, he'd kept Chaucer moving most days. He needed to see about getting another horse, so he could switch them out and not have to work them so hard. "I'll try not to be long."

He'd unharness Chaucer and put him in the small

pasture to graze if Esther had an extra room. Of course, there was a cot on his side of the building, and as tired as he was, the cot would be like sleeping on a bed of hay.

He spotted Esther sitting at a sewing machine, pushing fabric through the foot feed, and memories washed over him. Some good. Some bad. But seeing the focused smile on his aunt's face outweighed any troubled memories he might have. He turned the knob and stepped inside. "Hello."

"Malachi," Esther said. "You're home."

"Hi," April said from the floor the moment his gaze touched hers. Jeb lay on a blanket just within her reach, kicking his hands and feet in the air. A sense of home and rightness settled on his shoulders. The same feeling he'd hoped to have one day whenever he drove home from Abe's home after dinner with all the *kinder* running around. Part of him envied Abe's blessings, while the other part knew a house full of family was something he would never have. But now, seeing those closest to his heart, including the small redheaded woman, round with a *boppli* in her belly, he felt more than slight envy for a family he never thought he would have. He hungered for it, like a man too long without sustenance. Hoped for it. And, *Gotte* help him, he'd even prayed for it this morning on the drive to Mr. Bassett's.

He pulled his mind from his thoughts and refocused on April. Was she mopping the floors again? If so, she was thorough, and he didn't see a bucket of water. Still, she was working hard at whatever she was doing. He'd have to make certain she didn't work so hard tomorrow. He was about to ask her reason for the task when Aunt

Esther shuffled in front of him, took his hand, and led him to his *mamm*'s old worktable.

"Look at the wonders April worked."

He noted the pieces of fabric laid out, ready to be sewn. "*Jah*, it's nice. It'll make a *wunderbar* blanket for the *boppli*."

"No," Aunt Esther said as she began stacking the squares. "The table."

The walnut top gleamed with a glossy shine. The deep scratches left from its use as a worktable and the watermarks were gone. He crouched and inspected the legs, looking for a gouge he'd made when he was a child building a birdhouse with his *daed*'s tools. He'd missed his intended mark and struck the table. He unfolded and found April watching him. It was an old table his *grossdaddi* had made for his *grossmammi* when his *mamm* had been a child. It was never meant to be used as a dining table, but April's restoration had him thinking about cutting it down and taking it to his house. He rubbed his hand over the smooth top, searching for any hint of the deep gouges. "You did well," he said.

"The table looks better than when my *bruder* made it," Aunt Esther said as she laid her fabric pieces onto the table then took her spot back at the sewing table.

"How did you do it?" Malachi asked.

April climbed to her knees, and he rushed over to help her to her feet. He reached for her hand, and she easily took his. He felt the raised scars from her burns, still smooth with new skin, but those weren't what caused his pulse to skip a beat and his breath to hitch. It was her. This lovely, *wunderbar* woman with a heart big enough to love a *boppli* not her own and an aging woman whose mind darted in and out of reality as her own family. But was it big enough to love a man like him, too?

He clenched his jaw against the unwarranted thought as he helped her to her feet.

She bent over, picked up a Mason jar from the floor, and handed it to him. He unscrewed the lid and brought it to his nose. He couldn't place the smell, but it reminded him of his aunt's baking. "What is it?"

"Walnut shells." She smiled. "We spent some time cracking shells in preparation for one of the pies earlier. I pounded them, ground them to a powder, mixed it with watered-down glue, and then pressed them into the cracks. We let it dry, buffed the roughness out and then coated it with coconut oil. I'm working on some of the more noticeable spots on the floor now."

"And it works?" he asked, looking at where she'd been sitting to see the work in progress. His own skepticism annoyed him. He glanced around and noticed areas where holes had once been and were no longer. It obviously had worked. The table looked good. The floors looked better.

April shrugged.

"You don't know if it works?" He laughed as he rubbed his hand over his clean yet prickly jaw. He'd shaved this morning, but the day had been long.

"My *daed* did some woodworking. I saw him do this with sawdust, so I thought why not give this a try. I guess time will tell if it works or not, *jah*?"

"I guess so," he said, laughing. "You're resourceful. I'll give you that."

"Denki." She glanced down at her hands, twisting them as if she was nervous. "How is your friend?"

He touched her arm, drawing her gaze to his. "He is *gut*. A few stitches. No fingers lost. He just won't be working construction with me for a while."

"That is *gut* news, Malachi," Aunt Esther said.

"*Jah*," April said, bobbing her chin. "Will his absence cause you more problems with your clients?"

"Levi's *bruder* will fill the gap until I can find a permanent replacement," he said, pleased with her concern. "He's *gut* with a hammer. Better than Uri, but Abe has a farm, a new *fraa* and a *boppli*."

"That is *gut*. I'd offer to help, but I think I have my hands full here," she said with a teasing wink.

"I'd say you're doing more than enough to help out."

"Come, sit." April motioned to a chair. "I'll pour you some coffee."

It was then he noticed the cookstove. Free of dust, grime and rust, as it should be. "You two have been busy."

"It's been *gut* to keep my hands busy," she said. "It was difficult not to worry about you and your friend."

He narrowed his eyes as she handed him the cup. *Worry?* When was the last time he had anyone share his burdens? He couldn't remember. He wasn't certain anyone ever had. Levi was right. April was different. Was she different enough to ignore his past?

"I am thankful," April said. "And before you ask, *jah*,

I moved some boxes upstairs, but I only carried what I felt comfortable carrying. The rest are in the closet."

"I'm thankful you did not fall managing the stairs," he said. "I wouldn't forgive myself if something happened to you or the *boppli*."

"I promise, I was careful. I have too much to do to be laid up by another accident." She paused as she looked at her hands. She brought one of her hands up to her face and pushed a curl back beneath her *kapp*. She moistened her lips. "When we get a moment, I need to speak with you," she whispered as she looked across the room at Aunt Esther.

"You've done well giving her something to do."

"*Denki*," April said as she sat on a stool across from him. "Purpose is *gut* for the mind. Although she's had a few slips in the last few days, but that is not what I wish to speak to you about."

The way she fidgeted with her hands, he had a sneaking suspicion he wasn't going to like what she was about to say, but ignoring the conversation would not make her pressing thoughts go away. "You're not leaving Garnett, are you?"

Something he couldn't explain tugged at his heart at the thought of her leaving. He'd become so used to seeing her every morning before work, and every evening for dinner when he returned to pick up Jeb. Where before he rushed from one task to the next with little pause, now he looked forward to meals and lingering at the table with April. And, of course, with Aunt Esther and Jeb, too.

"No, that's not it at all. Not unless you ask me to leave."

He knew the moment she said the words he wouldn't. He'd keep her around as long as she was willing. And sitting here with her, he was beginning to rethink the idea of finding her a husband. There wasn't an Amish man good enough for her. "All right, then," he said. "What is it you want to talk about?"

Once again, she glanced toward Aunt Esther as if she worried about how his aunt would react. "Your *bruder*, Jared."

The moment she said the words, the room grew chilly, and she second-guessed the wisdom of bringing up a sore subject. But Malachi needed to know. He sat forward in his chair cradling his cup of coffee in his hands. The pulse in his clenched jaw, much like she'd seen Jared's do earlier in the day, ticked furiously.

"I don't want to sound harsh, April, or hurt your feelings, but my *bruder* is none of your concern. I will not speak of him."

She inhaled a breath, and at the risk of emotionally being pushed away, climbed off the stool and laid her hand over Malachi's. "I understand."

He stood, forcing her hand to fall from his. "There is nothing to understand."

She chewed the inside of her cheek and debated whether to continue with the conversation. If she did, what words would she say? There was no way for it except to meet him head-on before he took up Jeb and left. If he did that without her being able to tell him, the truth would eventually come out, and then he'd wonder why she'd hidden it from him. "He was here."

His cheeks burned red with anger, but she didn't fear him, not like she had feared David when he was in a mood. Malachi wasn't upset with her and would not subject her to the brunt of his irritation. He was only upset with the situation. Strange how she knew this to be true with Malachi, when she had never been able to predict her late husband's volatile mood shifts. Instead of taking a step back, she stood her ground and even lifted her chin in a show of courage for herself. "Earlier this morning, before lunch, he was in your shop looking through papers on your desk."

Malachi speared his fingers along the side of his head so hard that she expected him to wince from the force. "What did he want?"

That was a question she'd mulled around in her head since this morning. She folded her hands in front of her and felt the dry patches along the crest of her scars. She must remember to apply ointment to them later. Her hands weren't used to scrubbing floors, not after having been merely useless for a few months while the open burns worked on closing and healing. "I don't know. He said nothing, and when I approached, he ran off."

Malachi's nostrils flared as he drew in and out air. He clenched and unclenched his fists. She'd seen angry men before, and seen them bluster, but she'd never seen a man work so hard to collect calm.

"I did not know it was Jared, not until later when I found him in Esther's living room." She paused at the fire in his eyes, unsure if she should say anything more.

"He favors you. I see that now. I hope you don't fire me, or ask me to leave, but I had been upstairs with Esther for a moment, and when I came back down to check on Jeb, Jared was there, holding him."

The color drained from Malachi's face. He looked at the child and scooped him up before sitting in the chair. Malachi's large palm rubbed Jeb's little back while his other palm cradled the *boppli*.

"He wasn't there to harm him or take him. At least, it didn't appear that way," she said. "I think he just wanted to see him, to see he was all right, and that you were all right, too."

The sound of the treadle pumping filled the space between them. Esther, busy with her sewing, was oblivious to the tension thicker than a fall fog hanging in the room. And, April hoped, deaf to the conversation.

"I should have kept better watch."

Malachi shook his head. "You could not have known. *I* couldn't have known."

"I'm sorry," she said, more for the obvious ache owning his heart.

"There is nothing to be sorry for, April," he said. "I wonder how many times I've left Jeb in a room while I tended to other things. Jared could have been there any of those times. The truth is, Jeb is not mine. If Jared were to take him, there is nothing I could do."

She recalled the sadness in Jared's eyes. The tears he'd tried to hide from her, and the kiss to Jeb's brow. "Again, he said nothing, but I got a sense he loves this child and knows you're the best thing for Jeb."

Even though the clunks and creaks of the treadle as

Esther worked diligently on her project filled the room, silence held them for a few moments. April wanted to fill it with useless chatter, but she allowed the quiet to remain. She didn't want her words to press him into conversation if he wasn't ready or willing.

"Did my *bruder* look well?"

The worry in his voice tugged on April's heart, but she would not lie. "No. I can't say he did. He looked hungry and tired." He'd looked like a ragged, starving fox ready to steal his next meal. "I sent him away with some food, and he gave his thanks. I hope that doesn't upset you."

"How could it, April?" His Adam's apple bobbed. Emotion filled his eyes. "Does not *Gotte*'s word say, 'For I was an hungered, and ye gave me meat: I was thirsty, and ye gave me drink: I was a stranger, and ye took me in: Naked, and ye clothed me: I was sick, and ye visited me: I was in prison, and ye came unto me'?"

She stared at him, unable to respond. The things she'd done for Jared had come without a second thought. It was out of love for another human being. And she was certain she would offer him food again, even if Malachi told her not to. "As we all should, *jah*?"

The emotion filling his eyes leaked from the corners and slid down his clean-shaven cheek. "*Jah*, but many don't. Not among our community. It is not always our way. My brother has been inspected with a magnifying glass and found lacking. He is not worthy of kindness or compassion." He paused, his gaze seeking hers. "Yet you gave it to him. I wonder if it's because he was a stranger to you. If you knew the trouble he's caused, if his trouble affected you in some way, would you still have showed him such grace?"

She touched her fingers to Jeb's downy head. "Jared's actions have impacted me. Not in the same way as you and Esther, or the *gmay*, but still, if not for the abandonment of this child by his father, I wouldn't have the blessing of holding him and loving him as he deserves."

"You are a wonder, April," Malachi said. "Your life has not been easy, yet somehow you see sunshine and flowers in the footsteps behind you."

She shook her head. "That is where you are wrong, Malachi. The ground behind me where I have walked has been worked and plowed. Some of the ground where I have left my footprints have left their own mark upon the soles of my feet and even bigger marks on my heart."

That deep ache she'd carried since the fire somehow no longer reminded her of grief's presence. She swiped at her eyes with the backs of her hands and sniffed, knowing without a doubt that coming to Garnett had been *Gotte*'s will. She wasn't sure what that would look like in a year, or even tomorrow, but if the loss of her childhood community and her family, the difficulties in her marriage, and Samantha and David's deaths in the fire had brought her here to this man—to give him a hope for a future he could not see because he was blinded by his own past—then it would all be worth it because it would be *Gotte*'s doing. Even if she'd made her own detours and taken her own paths, *Gotte*, in His grace and mercy for her and Malachi, had brought her here.

"Seed has been sown, Malachi, but those seeds

haven't always sprouted. The sunshine and flowers are what I see ahead of me. It is what I hope to see, touch and smell. Life on this earth is tenuous. It is nothing more than a flash of lightning. One moment we are here, the next we are gone. How I treat others matters to me. I want my legacy, to be how I loved others. I will not say I haven't looked back and for a moment held a grudge for what was and what wasn't and what I thought my life should be, but this life is not mine alone. All *Gotte*'s creatures are worthy of kindness and compassion. Their worthiness is not up to me, it is *Gotte* given." Even David had been deserving of those things. Had she withheld them from her late husband? The past was nothing she could change, only the future. "Don't you agree?" she asked, wondering what Malachi's thoughts were on the matter.

She'd seen kindness. Had known it. But she'd also experienced the horrors of disservice. The community she'd grown up in had turned its backs on her when she married outside of it. Its members had shunned her for not seeking a man in the community and threatened to shun her *daed* if he didn't cut her off. Making her return home after David's death more difficult and, in her mind, impossible. Losing her family, friends and the community she'd known all her life had been almost as bad as her most recent loss. If not for her sweet Samantha, it would have been. Yet, the community where she was a mere stranger offered her a place to live while she healed from her wounds. Some in it might have tried to marry her off again, but no one threatened to shun her if she didn't comply, even after it was well known she was pregnant.

"Generally, I would say *jah*," he said. "But I fear that is not the case with my *bruder*. He has made his choice, and until he makes amends to the elders and to the *gmay*, any association with Jared would be cause for speculation, even out of a compassionate heart." He laid Jeb in the crook of his arm and gazed down at the *boppli*. Even in Malachi's distress, love for the child illuminated his eyes. The tone of his skin glowed with affection. She recalled what Esther had said earlier about Malachi's life not being easy. He'd lost both parents, and she suspected he still carried those wounds in his heart. "We must consider the *gmay* as one. How would the outside world perceive us if it saw us accepting behaviors that go against the order? We cannot think of oneself alone but of each other as a whole."

She clenched her teeth on the inside of her cheek.

David's compassion for others, or really anything for that matter, had not existed outside of his own self-centeredness. He loved, but never anyone or anything more than his own self-satisfaction. He offered gifts, but only when he expected a greater gift in return. Once he'd brought her flowers, delicate and beautiful, from the field. She'd been taken back by the gesture. Until he'd turned on her when she couldn't give in to his wishes.

"I understand. I was asked to never return to the community I grew up in upon my decision to marry David. No one there was happy I married outside our community, but I felt circumstances dictated my choices."

He grabbed her hand and squeezed. "I am sorry for that, but if you want to make connections in Garnett and keep them pleasant, be careful associating with my *bruder* or you'll be shunned."

She looked around the space she'd spent all day cleaning and preparing. Her own business. A place where she could sell goods and support herself and her *boppli*. Would offering food to the hungry cause her to lose her dream?

"You've showed more kindness to a stranger than most within our community show to their loved ones. You are rare, April Beiler, and I'm sorry my cousin did not see the gift he had for a wife." He squeezed her hand again before releasing her. "I wouldn't like it if that kindness caused you ill as well."

Chapter Ten

Malachi patted Jeb's back until he fell back to sleep. Once his nephew's eyes remained closed longer than a full minute and his breathing evened out, Malachi crawled back into bed, but he wasn't sure he could sleep, especially considering he'd been wide awake when Jeb had stirred for his bottle.

He kept thinking about his brother and April. She was *wunderbar*, but Jared's current situation was dangerous. He'd heard rumors about his brother. He'd even had an officer recently come out to the house asking about Jared, which set had set his heart hammering with fear. Three years earlier Jared had been drinking while racing his buggy against Nathan Zook, another young Amish man set on finding trouble. Their buggies ended up tangled with an *Englischer's* car and Delphine Beachy paralyzed. Any rumors after, Malachi didn't know what was true and what wasn't, but until he knew for certain, he didn't like Jared coming near Jeb or April. Jared's bad choices had already negatively impacted more lives than he should. But April was also stubborn, and brash, qualities many Amish men would find unsuitable in a *fraa.* The fact she cared enough for a man who was obvious trouble to give him food, a stranger who could have harmed her, spoke volumes to him.

Still, he'd have to speak to her and caution her against helping Jared any further. Help would only encourage him to return, and that wasn't something Malachi wanted until his brother received the help he needed.

Turning on his side, Malachi caught a glimpse of the moon shining through the window he had yet to cover with curtains. Since it had only been him living here until Jeb had been deposited on his doorstep, he hadn't taken care to have curtains made. Normally, that was something a wife would do, but he didn't have one, and he hadn't wanted to burden Aunt Esther or his cousin's *fraa* with the task. April would do it, if he asked, but he was already beholden to her for seeing to his aunt's care, as well as Jeb's. And if he were honest with himself, the care of him, too.

He covered his eyes with his forearm and groaned. What was he going to do? "*Gotte*, You know why I can't marry. No woman would have me. No woman would trust me when the men in my family have proven untrustworthy."

April would. The thought came without his permission. Or his wanting. That wasn't true. If he could marry, he wouldn't have second thoughts; since her marriage to his cousin hadn't been easy or kind, he would not subject her to the speculation of his past, even if he was blameless.

"There is nothing to be done but to revisit the list," he whispered. Jeb groaned, mirroring the ache in Malachi's chest. If his life had been different—if his father hadn't been cast out of the church and his mother hadn't given in to her depression and committed suicide—then maybe he could promise April a *gut* life.

He slid out from beneath the covers and grabbed the flashlight from the nightstand. He laid his palm on Jeb's chest and smiled at the rise and fall. April was right. This life was tenuous. Every day was a gift. And every day he had with those he loved was a miracle. "Sleep well, little one."

Malachi turned the wick down on the oil lamp and tiptoed out of the room and toward the dining table. He switched on the flashlight then lit the chandelier hanging above the small dining table he rarely used, pulled out the single, lone chair, and sat on the hard seat.

Silence clung to the walls, leaving the pounding of his pulse to reign. He'd never paid attention to the difference between the four chairs surrounding Aunt Esther's small dining table and the sole chair at his. Had he set himself apart and made himself a hermit? *Jah*, he had. Inviting anyone too close into his life left him vulnerable.

His Bible remained where he'd left it last Sunday. The sight of the black-leather cover reminded him of the passage where he'd left off. While the entire community had been at church, he'd sat here, contemplating ten words.

It is not good that the man should be alone.

He squeezed his eyes closed and inhaled a long, calming breath.

Abe had suggested Malachi begin with Genesis and

find gratitude for all *Gotte* had done. Creating the heavens and the earth, the animals, the moon, sun and the stars. The fruits of the land. And then he'd come to that passage. The one about man not being alone.

Malachi had read that same passage for the last several weeks. The first week, he'd walked away, frustrated by his reaction to the words. How could so few words cause regret and anger the way they had? The next week, while the entire community had rested and visited each other, Malachi had opened the Bible and contemplated the words. He'd sobbed at his ungratefulness. Every time he'd opened the passage after that, he'd written down the things he was thankful for that made him feel not alone.

He slid the Bible across the table and opened it to where the folded paper poked out from the edges. He touched the paper, drawing his hand over the smooth surface. Knowing by his imperfect memory the names listed. Jeb and Aunt Esther were at the top of that list, as were his cousins and their families. And even though he hadn't been to church in a few services, the community had helped him when he'd needed them. Bishop Mueller and the deacons often checked in on him, their wives leaving gift baskets for him and Jeb. He'd written every name of his customers who had given work, both small and large, thankful they'd trusted him to build their porches, homes and workshops. They'd provided him with a means to support himself, Jeb and Aunt Esther.

He thanked *Gotte* for each of them and thanked *Gotte* for the blessings he'd bestowed upon him. Especially

Aunt Esther, who'd taken two young boys under her care when she didn't have to.

At the bottom of the paper was his brother's name. Somehow, he'd been able to forgive Jared and be thankful that he'd brought Jeb to him and not left him with an *Englischer.* And he'd thanked *Gotte* for the mother who'd given Jeb life. One day, he hoped to learn her story, to share it with Jeb.

He had many blessings and much to be thankful for.

Pulling the Bible closer, he leaned his elbows against the table and stared at the passage. Genesis 2:18. *It is not good that the man should be alone; I will make him an help meet for him.*

An ache formed in his chest. He'd never begrudged the way of things in his life. Never wanted anything different than he'd had. Moved through every day with the sole purpose of doing what needed to be done with as little emotional attachment as possible. And now, thanks to the redheaded Amish woman who'd stormed into his place of business nearly a week ago demanding she rent him the open space next door, he wanted more. For the first time since he'd found his *mamm* motionless on her bed, without breath in her lungs, he wanted more.

He wanted a *fraa*. He wanted April.

The rooster's call pulled him from his musings. Early morning light filtered through the windows, illuminating the blank, empty spaces of his home. Other than the kitchen, which was filled with cabinets, a cookstove and a sink, there was little in his house. There'd been no need. Once he'd completed building his home, he'd spent little time here. It had been a place for him to eat, sleep and clean up. He hadn't planned on needing to move in Aunt Esther or having a child who would need a nurturing home. A child who would benefit from April's care.

He pushed from the chair, slid it back under the table and, on his silent, stockinged feet, slipped inside his bedroom. He checked on Jeb, dressed, checked on Jeb again, and donned his hat before heading outside to do the morning chores.

The coop door squeaked and the hens squawked as he ducked inside. "Good morning, lovelies. *Denki* for the fruits of your labor."

Hay pricked his hand as he slipped it beneath the feathers of one hen, searching for an egg. By the time he was done, he had more than a dozen eggs. He'd leave a few here for himself and take the rest to Aunt Esther when he drove into town.

Laying down the basket on the outdoor worktable, he trudged to the barn to feed and water the horses. By the time he was done, the sun had peaked over the horizon. He walked back to the house where he shucked off his boots at the front door and washed up. He halted at the small round table and turned the Bible toward him. He glanced around his sparsely furnished home. Dull and drab without life. There was no calendar, no clock, no curtains. So much like the home he'd grown up in as his *mamm* fell into despair. Even though they had curtains in his childhood home, the only time they were opened was when Aunt Esther arrived with her cheery, sunny presence, and stirred *Mamm* from her slumber.

A soft coo sang from the bedroom and Malachi

shook off the ennui cloaking his shoulders. He pushed open the door and peeked into the crib. Jeb's little feet and fisted hands pumped the air. As soon as his nephew spotted Malachi, his face brightened with pure happiness.

Malachi rubbed his chin. "Forgive me, *Gotte*, for slipping into sadness. Thank You for this *boppli*, who makes me smile."

He needed to focus on the good. He needed to choose joy. If not for himself, then for Jeb. The *boppli* deserved better. He deserved a *mamm* like April, even if Malachi didn't deserve a *gut* Amish wife.

Malachi lifted Jeb into his arms and patted his back. "Well, little one, do you think we have it in us to court April?"

Or was she determined to never marry again?

April's pulse sped at the sound of buggy wheels on the gravel in the alleyway and she couldn't help the smile taking over her.

"We have visitors," Esther said from the rocking chair. "I wonder who it could be."

That piqued April's curiosity. She hadn't expected Malachi this morning, but the buggy's arrival made her think it couldn't be anyone else.

April rolled the dough into a ball and covered it with a flour cloth. By the time she'd washed and dried her hands, Esther was already out of the rocker and shuffling across the room. "Oh, it's Malachi and Jeb. What a surprise. Looks like he has eggs."

"*Gut*," April said as she stood next to Esther's shoulder. "We're almost out, and it'll save us from having to go to the store before Wednesday."

With Malachi coming every morning for breakfast, they had gone through more eggs than Esther claimed they needed, but then, April was an added mouth, too. At least she didn't feel like a burden here. Not that her father's new wife ever had made her feel like one, but April saw how the portions on every plate had become smaller over time, and no matter how much she'd helped out at the farm and in her *daed*'s woodworking shop, she had rarely felt she worked enough to compensate for the food she ate.

"Do you think he has to work?" April asked, wondering about Malachi's appearance.

"Oh, no. He wouldn't work on Sunday," Esther said. "He won't even carry that awful thing he talks to. Still, mighty strange he's here on a Sunday since we don't have church service, today."

"I hope nothing is wrong with Jeb." Worry about the baby sent April out the kitchen door. She lengthened her stride and didn't stop until she stood in front of Malachi. "Is Jeb all right?"

She took the baby from him and felt his forehead with the back of her hand. Then she kissed his little round cheek. She looked up at Malachi, his brow furrowed.

"*Jah*, he is fine," he said, and held up the basket. "We have eggs."

"Mmm," she said, turning toward the house. "And you couldn't have waited until tomorrow? Esther says you never come on Sundays."

She heard him laugh. “Is that so? I guess we’re making an exception today. I hope you don’t mind. Jeb missed you?”

“Is that so?” she asked, repeating his earlier question. “And what about his *daed*?”

She regretted the words the moment they were out. She didn’t want him to think she’d changed her mind about marriage. She hadn’t, even though she’d thought about spending time with Malachi. Even during tough conversations like they’d had last night.

“I’d be lying if I said I didn’t, but that’s not why I’ve come,” he said. “I want to talk to you, but we can do that later.”

He opened the screen door for her and waited until she stepped inside. April laid Jeb down on a blanket spread out in front of the window, where he’d get plenty of sunshine. She turned in time to watch Malachi sweep off his hat and hang it on the coat tree beside the door. He fluffed his brown hair with his fingers. The locks were long and soft with golden glints, as if the sun kissed him each day. He bent down and bussed Esther’s cheek. “How are you on this *gut* morning, Aunt Esther?”

“Well,” she said. “I’m surprised to see you. I hope everything is okay.”

“Yes, all is well. I even stopped by Uri’s to see what I could help with while Emmaline kept Jeb for me,” he said as he set the basket of eggs on the table. “The hens outdid themselves and I thought I would bring fresh eggs. With all the cooking April’s been doing, feeding me in the mornings, it’s the least I can do.”

April appreciated the gift, and she felt guilty for wondering what he wanted in return, especially since he didn't make her feel like a burden by coming into town. She took up the basket and looked under the towel, amazed at the number of eggs inside. "This is *wunderbar*!"

"I'll bring more tomorrow." He winked at her. "Since I eat here most mornings, I don't need them. That is, as long as you don't mind cooking."

"Oh, not at all. I enjoy cooking." She had lost her enjoyment of it for a while, but seeing the appreciation on Malachi's face as he took his first bite of every meal she made, had renewed her love for cooking. It was almost like she had a sense of purpose, to bring a smile to Malachi's face through his stomach.

"With April getting ready to open the store, she'll need every egg she can get. Soon she'll be the talk of the town, and everyone will be asking for her pies."

April couldn't help noticing Malachi's uncomfortable shift of his feet. Was he having second thoughts about her store? He said he'd come here to talk to her. Was it about the store? She hoped not, because even though she liked cooking for him, she didn't want to give up her dream. Too much was at stake for her and her *boppli*.

What if Malachi sent her away? What if she married him and he left her, like David had? What then? She'd have no home and no means to care for herself. She wouldn't allow that to happen again if she could help it. If Malachi had changed his mind about the store, then she'd have no other choice but to find another place to rent, even if it was from an *Englischer*.

She spent the next hour kneading loaves of bread, letting them rise, and baking them. During the rising time and baking time, she, Malachi and Esther peeled and sliced apples.

She prepared a bowl of water and lemon juice and placed it in the middle of the table. Esther didn't have a fancy apple corer and slicer, so they did it all the old-fashioned way. She'd told Malachi it was good to keep her hands busy, and it was true. However, she couldn't help wondering about the coming conversation.

"The store is coming along," Esther said. "It'll be open in no time. Nan did a great job, too."

April looked up from the apple she was peeling and noticed Malachi's pale face and worried frown. "Nan?"

"I think Esther meant you, April." Malachi scraped the sliced apples from his plate into the bowl and took up another one with a trembling hand.

"Oh, dear," Esther said. "I did it again. I am sorry. I guess I haven't been this excited about anything since Nan opened the sewing shop. Malachi's *mamm* had a gift for sewing."

April sucked in a sharp breath. No wonder Malachi looked like he was going to be ill. She reached across the table and touched his hand, drawing his eyes to her. She willed him to lean on her strength until the moment passed.

"No need to apologize, Esther. We all make those kinds of mistakes. But seeing your work, I wonder if Malachi's *mamm* learned her skills from you," April said, trying to divert her focus. "You finished that quilt top in no time, and it's lovely. Maybe we can work on the other this afternoon."

"No," Esther said. "Today, we enjoy each other. No work."

April didn't see quilting as work, but she didn't want to mention it in case Esther's mind was in another time and place.

Jeb began to fuss from the blanket on the floor. She and Malachi both moved to get him at the same time.

"Like Esther said, no work," Malachi said, dropping his hand on her shoulder as if to encourage her to sit back down.

"Jeb is not work. He is pure enjoyment," April reminded him as she stood up. "Honestly, my hands could use a break from the peeling and slicing."

At her words, he looked at her hands. He took one in his and lifted it. She tried to pull away, but he held her firm as he inspected the healing scars. "I'm sorry. You shouldn't be working your hands so hard."

"That is not an option." Pulling her hand back, she smiled. "What I can do is take breaks by holding Jeb for a spell."

He didn't argue. He let her go, but she felt his hesitation.

"I'm fine," she said. "The apples are almost done, if you don't mind helping Esther finish?"

She knelt beside Jeb and changed his diaper. Her own *boppli* stirred in her belly, and she took delight knowing soon she'd have two babies to care for and keep her days full of sunshine. She fed him, burped him and played with him until the bread was ready to come out of the oven. That's when she placed him back on the blanket to entertain himself.

The moment she set the bread out on the cooling racks, Malachi was there in front of her with a Mason jar in his hand. He led her to the dining table, motioned for her to sit, and took the chair next to her. She looked around and found Esther playing with Jeb on the floor.

"Coconut oil. It's not much, but I hope it will help soothe the chapped skin, and you should wear gloves when mopping the floors, or let me do them."

She started to laugh, but then he took her hand in his and began massaging lotion onto her skin. She dared to look at his face, and she wasn't sure what she saw there. All she knew was, she couldn't recall anyone taking care of her in this way, not since her *mamm* had passed away, and she didn't want to tell him she had her salve cream she made for her burns. Instead, she allowed him to rub the oil into her skin.

"I won't lecture you. I don't think you would heed my advice anyway," he said as he winked. "But I do ask you take care of yourself, too. Esther needs you. Jeb needs you. Your *boppli* will need you. And," he said as he finally looked up at her, "I need you. If you don't take care of your hands, it'll be hard to take care of us, and to bake all those pies you intend on selling."

For the first time since he'd said they needed to talk, she began to relax. "You're not going to tell me I can't have the store?"

Malachi shook his head. "No, not unless you don't want it."

She looked over her shoulder and noticed Esther's

focus was still on Jeb. "What did you want to talk about?"

He rubbed the excess lotion into his hands and sat back in the dining chair. "Two things. The first, I hope you listen carefully."

She swallowed the emotion in her throat. "Okay."

"First, I appreciate what you did for my brother. It speaks to your character and the loving individual you are. I have no regrets about hiring you to care for Aunt Esther and Jeb."

She flinched at the word *hire* but pushed it aside because that's what she was: hired help, and not family as she'd grown to think of them as, including Malachi.

"However, there is a possibility Jared could be dangerous." He leaned forward and pressed his elbows onto the table, folding his hands beneath his chin. "I don't pay attention to gossip, but an officer did stop by my place a few weeks ago looking for my brother."

The man she'd seen had been scared and hungry, but she had seen him rifling through Malachi's papers. What had he been looking for? Money? Something else?

"I will be careful," she said. "I'm not going to lie, I was scared when I'd seen him both times, and I wouldn't have offered him anything if I hadn't known he was your brother. What is the second thing you want to talk to me about?"

"Well, there's no easy way about this, so I'm just going to come out and ask," he said as he rose and began pacing before stopping to look at her. "Will you be my wife?"

"Why?"

Malachi opened and closed his mouth like a fish left on the bank, seeking water. "Why, what?"

She eased from her chair and rubbed her stomach as she stood.

Malachi eyed her like a rattlesnake about to strike and took a step back.

Gut.

"You asked me to be your wife, and I want to know why." She'd married the wrong man for the wrong reasons once already, and she didn't want to do it again. Malachi's kindness had tempted her to change her mind about marrying again, but when he'd asked her the question, she immediately knew she had to know his reason. There were no pretty words or flowers, not that she wanted those things, but there hadn't been a hint that he wanted a wife. After protesting all of Esther's attempts at getting them to the altar, April was curious.

"Why not?" He answered her question with a question of his own.

She clenched her teeth. Frustration heated her nostrils as she blew out air. In the short time she'd known Malachi, she'd come to care for him. After last night, when they had an honest discussion, she thought she might love him. This morning as he soothed lotion into her tender wounds, she was fairly certain she probably did love him, but she wouldn't accept his blunt proposal if she didn't have an inkling he felt the same. "Because you don't want a wife, and I don't want a husband." Not one who couldn't love her, or at the least offer her some affection. She propped her hands on her hips. "That's why not."

"What if I've changed my mind?"

When? How? Those questions ambushed her like a hound on a squirrel. Now that the store was almost ready for business, did he want to use it for his own purposes? Was his intent in proposing to her to keep her occupied as a wife so she couldn't have her own business?

"Have you changed your mind?"

His hesitation told her all she needed to know. The obstinate man didn't want a wife, which meant he had an ulterior motive.

"Never mind," she said as she held up her hand and shook her head. "I can see that you don't. And if the intention behind your proposal is to get me to change my mind about opening the store, I won't. I will open my store, if not here, then somewhere else. If you won't rent to me, then I'll find another person who will."

He reached for her, but she jerked her arm away. She would not be enticed by affection to bend to his will. She couldn't.

"April, please," he said, his voice soft, but she heard it over the pounding in her ears. "That's not it."

She narrowed her gaze and waited for him to explain. "Go on."

He crossed his arms and shifted from one foot to the other. "You're right, I don't want a wife. There are things about my past that make it impossible for me to marry. But after spending the last week with you, I've found that a union between us could be beneficial, like a business deal, and for that I could change my mind."

"A business deal?" A pain in her heart reverberated through her entire body. Tears sprung and streamed from the corners of her eyes. She wiped them dry and willed the rest of the tears pressing on her lashes to remain where they were. When she'd married David, she'd known he didn't love her. Their marriage had been an arrangement, but she'd hoped affection would grow between them, and once Samantha was born, she'd realized her marriage wouldn't even be agreeable. In that, she'd made her bed and had to lie in it, but she'd learned her lesson.

"Jah."

If he had asked her two days ago, or even last night, she probably would have married him. Then they would have at least been equally yoked in their affection for each other. But today, knowing now her affection was more than that, all because he'd showed her kindness and affection by caring for her hands, she couldn't marry him.

"No," she said. "If you don't mind keeping Esther company, I'd like to go for a walk."

Before he answered, she slipped outside and stalked down the stairs.

Chapter Eleven

Malachi pounded the hammer with such force, he bent the nail. He sat back on his heels and growled before pulling out the nail and tossing it into the bucket.

"Wow," Levi said. "Whenever Abe abuses a nail, it's usually because he's had a disagreement with Naomi and he's lost. But since you don't have a *fraa* and you're not courting, it makes me wonder what has you frustrated and beating nails like they stole your favorite dog."

"I don't have a dog."

"When I become a dog breeder, you'll have first pick. Every family needs a dog," Levi said.

"Not me," Malachi snorted and glanced down at the bucket of nails he'd ruined so far this morning, knowing he'd work on straightening them out later, and grunted. It had been a little more than a month since he'd asked April to marry him, and he couldn't stop replaying her reply in his head. Of course, she was still in mourning, which is one reason he'd proposed the way he had. Dry and businesslike. Like writing up a contract with one of his clients. The only things missing were the line items of expectations and cost, and signatures. What kind of fool was he? "Would you believe my hens have me working triple time in the mornings?"

"Sounds like a good problem to have." Levi held a piece of plywood against the two-by-four frame with his forearm and hammered a nail to pin it in place. "The good news is, you only have a handful of nails along the bottom to secure."

"I think you've missed your calling as a comedian, Levi," he said. "Too many eggs aren't a problem if you have a large family to feed. But I don't. It's just me."

Ever since April's obvious displeasure with him, he'd skipped breakfast, quietly accepted lunch, and made his excuses for not having dinner once he picked up Jeb. They barely spoke to each other than the business like report she gave him on how Jeb and Aunt Esther's day had been. The tension between him and April was awkward, and soon, if they didn't figure things out, he'd find another nanny for Jeb, which might be best anyway since April would be busy with her store.

"You could always ask April to sell the excess in her store," he said. "When does she open?"

"In two days." Malachi had bit the answer out harder than he'd like. "And she isn't talking to me." He clenched his jaw. He'd said too much, and now the entire Dienner family would know his business.

"Mmm," Levi said, forcing Malachi to glance at him.

"What do you mean 'mmm'?"

"Seems to me, you've divulged the real reason for the offense against the nails." Levi tsked. "Those poor nails."

Levi laughed, which annoyed Malachi even more than he already was.

"I don't think that's the problem. What does it matter if she's talking to me or not?" Except it did. He missed her smiles and their conversations. He missed her support of him even when he didn't need it. "The hens are producing so many eggs, I have to get up half an hour earlier to get Jeb ready and out the door in time to drop him off with Aunt Esther."

"Ah," Levi teased. "You're not talking to April either. I'm guessing you're not just leaving Jeb alone with our aunt in her old age."

"I don't want to talk about it." Malachi focused on swinging the hammer with the right pressure to keep the nail from folding over.

"Why isn't she speaking to you?" Levi asked.

Malachi glared at him.

"All right," Levi said. "I won't press, but if I were you, I'd do everything to get on her good side if you want any of her pie. Besides, she's watching Jeb. I'm no expert on women, but you'll have to talk sooner or later."

Yeah, he was afraid of that. And he had no idea what to say to her. He wasn't even sure why she wasn't speaking to him. Most women would be pleased at being proposed to. But then, April wasn't most women. She was different. One of a kind. Rare.

Before he knew what he was doing, he blurted, "I asked her to marry me."

Levi quit hammering. "You what?"

Malachi spun on the balls of his feet to look at his

cousin and rose to his full height. He lifted his hat from his head and raked his fingers through his damp hair. The air was hot and humid. He'd put in more effort bending nails, as Levi had claimed, than normal, making him hot and grumpy. So much so, he'd dropped his armor. "I asked her to marry me. She said no."

"Did she give a reason?"

Malachi thought back to the conversation and came up with nothing. "No. She only asked me why."

Levi took a drink from his canister then wiped the back of his hand over his forehead. "A reasonable question. What'd you tell her?"

"That I thought it would be beneficial, like a business deal." As he said the words aloud, he knew they sounded cold and less than appealing. He probably would have said no, too, if asked in such a way.

"Is that the only reason you asked her?"

What was Levi getting at? "What other reason would there be?"

"I don't know," Levi said. "Maybe because you love her."

"Whoa!" Malachi held up his hands. "Love? Outside of Jeb and Aunt Esther, I don't know what that emotion is. I didn't have the best examples growing up."

"You're preaching to the wrong man, there, Malachi."

Guilt ate at him for his self-centeredness. "I know, Levi, I'm sorry. I just don't have it in me to give my heart to any woman when she would resent me for what my father did." And what his *mamm* had done, too.

"You're not your father, Malachi. Just like Abe and I aren't our father."

"Except, you found out the man who raised you wasn't your father. My father's blood runs through my veins. He was unfaithful. He left our mother. And when given a choice, he left the church. What kind of man does that? What kind of man does that make me? And how would April…" he said, choking back the emotion filling his throat. "How would any woman react when they discover the truth about my past?"

"A man who only loves himself and his desires. You're not that man. And any woman worth loving would know that."

Levi's words struck a chord, hitting him directly in the chest.

"It's evident in the way you care for others and put people first. Aunt Esther, Jeb, Uri and April."

Malachi shook his head. "You weren't on the receiving end of the bishop's censure and the gossip when my father refused to kneel before the church and ask for forgiveness."

"I wasn't, Malachi, and I was far too young to understand," Levi said. "All I know is we can do better. We can treat others better."

"You sound like April." He smiled, his heart warming a little. "*Denki*, for talking. You've given me some things to consider."

The crunch of buggy wheels had Malachi turning toward the drive. It was Abe's buggy and horse. Had something happened at the other job site? He slid his hammer into his tool belt. "Your *bruder* made it."

"I won't speak about our conversation. You have my word," Levi said. "But if I were you, I would think about the reason for your marriage proposal. If you have any affection for April, or if there is a chance you could love her, you should tell her your past. Be honest and up front with her. If she's as good an Amish woman as I believe she is, she'll know you're not your father."

Wednesday morning came quicker than she'd expected, and she'd hardly slept the night before due to the excitement. She was finally flipping over the sign. Samatha's Collective was in business. After contemplating the name for her business, Esther had suggested she name the store after Samantha, and April couldn't think of anything better. It honored the life of her daughter and spoke to what April wanted to bring to the community. A store for everyone in the community to sell and buy goods.

She pulled apart the light blue curtains on the front door and the windows. Rain danced on the sidewalk outside and rivulets raced down the windows. Would the weather keep customers from coming?

Malachi hadn't even showed up with Jeb this morning, causing April to feel disappointed until Esther reminded her that Malachi didn't work on days like this, and probably wouldn't come to town. Still, she looked forward to seeing the *boppli* every day. Malachi too, even if tension made their encounters awkward.

"Esther, I suppose we may wait all day for our first customer," she said, turning the lock on the door and flipping the sign. "Especially with the rain, but we'll be here."

"Word gets around fast in this small town," Esther said. "I'm more worried you don't have enough pies for demand. I asked Malachi to let as many people know as possible."

April had barely spoken an entire sentence to Malachi since his proposal, four weeks and three days, which made her heart ache every day and with every avoided conversation. She missed their talks during breakfast and dinner. She missed him. His absence over the long weeks of bare conversations had given her little confidence that he'd told anyone about the store opening.

She'd waited on pins and needles the first few days after she'd told him she wouldn't marry him, wondering if he'd change his mind about renting the store to her. Honestly, though, she wasn't sure her business mattered much anymore if Malachi wasn't around. A part of her, desperate to secure a future for herself and the baby she would soon give birth to, saw no other way to survive. She couldn't trust any man had her best interest in mind, not when her late husband had placed his own wants and desires above anything else. The other part of her wanted to throw caution to the wind and accept Malachi's loveless offer, because she knew she loved him. The tension between them, the silence, made that fact more evident to her but fear kept her from allowing that love to sprout more than it had, and she couldn't confess her feelings for him.

For sure and certain, she kept telling herself love would come between her and Malachi with time, but she'd believed that with David, too, and it never had. At least not for him, not in the way April had expected love to manifest between a married couple. But then, their marriage had been nothing more than an arrangement between two people who wanted a spouse for their own reasons. David had felt it was time to start a family. She was relieving her father's house of an extra mouth to feed.

Fear held her captive, keeping her from accepting Malachi's proposal, even though her heart bent toward him in ways she'd never thought it would bend toward a man.

Now was not the time to dwell on love and marriage. Today was to be a celebration. She was seeing her dream come true. She lit the lantern above the worktable and dispelled more of the dark and dreariness from outside. "Would you like to sew today, or would you rather sit in rocker in the alcove and watch traffic?"

Esther shuffled toward the table and planted her small frame in the hard-back chair. "I have quilts to make, and they make my heart happy."

"Mine, as well, Esther," April said as she patted the older woman's hand. "I think I'll rearrange some items on the shelves."

They'd spent most of the past few weeks making jellies and jams and preparing premade spices to season meals. Friday, she'd made a few lavender-scented lotions as well as a few salves mixed with honey and myrrh for her hands. When Esther had discovered what April was creating, she'd suggested making some extra to sell, and she did, even as the jar of coconut oil Malachi had used remained by her bedside as a treasured moment. Every time she saw the jar she smiled with an achy heart and weepy eyes. Sunday, they'd baked breads and pies, and sweet butter with honey and cinnamon, and amazingly, during all that activity, April hadn't noticed any big slips with Esther's memory.

"There are a lot of empty spaces on the shelves," April said, trying not to worry. "Do you think I'm opening too soon?"

"No, dear. As word gets out about your intention with the store, the empty spaces will fill."

April hoped Esther was right. She hoped Samantha's Collective was so popular, she would need to hire help.

The bell above the door rang and April's focus moved from worry to excitement. Curious and hopeful about her first customer, she turned and found Malachi dipping through the door dripping wet from the rain. She rushed over and took Jeb from his hands, and after unbundling the *boppli*, she kissed his brow. "I missed you, little one."

She tugged the towel she used earlier to pat her and Esther dry after their trek from the house. She handed it to Malachi. He lifted his hat from his head and hung it on the hat tree she'd found tucked in a dusty corner. "It's good to see you."

"You, too," he said. "I wouldn't miss your opening day. Besides, I think it's the only way I may finally get a taste of your pie," he teased. "It's all I hear about from Levi, and I had some paperwork in the office to do, so I thought I'd put it off no more."

"I'd make you a pie if you ask," she said.

"Does this mean you're talking to me again?"

She sighed. "I was never not talking to you. I thought you were upset with me."

He shook his head. "No. Only frustrated with myself for not considering your wishes, which you made clear. I'm sorry for my proposal. It was thoughtless, and I should have had more consideration for you. You're still mourning. And, even if you weren't, you've made it known you don't want to marry again."

"I appreciate that you were honest about why you were asking, Malachi. Not many men would be as transparent." She wanted to be honest with him, too, but afraid of how he would respond, she held her tongue.

He started to say something, but his words were interrupted by the jingle of the bell. "It looks like you have another customer," he said, and held his hands out to take Jeb. "We'll talk later."

She dipped her chin. "I look forward to it."

She watched him as he disappeared through the French doors, her heart hammering in her chest. Her lack of courage to tell him how she felt about him frustrated her, and she regretted not saying anything. It would be easier if she pushed her feelings aside and told Malachi she'd changed her mind about his proposal. But she loved him, and that emotion thundered in her veins. It roared in her ears. If she told him she would marry him, would he see her love for him? Then what? He would rescind his offer. She would have to keep her distance to mere friendship, and that as a boss and employee.

"Hello," said a smiling woman in a dark blue dress

and a dark apron carrying a *boppli.* "I'm Naomi, Malachi's cousin's wife."

Esther jumped up from her treadle machine. "Oh, look at how this little one has grown in a few weeks. She favors you."

Naomi blushed. "*Denki.* It's good to see you, Esther. You should have Malachi bring you out to the farm for dinner, soon, and of course, you, too, April. The pie you sent home with Levi was *wunderbar.* I came to get another. But with the size of my family, I'll need at least two."

It was April's turn to blush. "I have them labeled. If you would like something a little different, one of the pies has jalapeños in it."

"Now that sounds interesting, something to keep my *mann* on his toes, *jah*?"

Laughter bubbled up in April's throat. "It's not as bad as that. The apples and cinnamon tone down the heat."

Naomi leaned forward and, in a whisper, said, "Honestly, I've really wanted to meet you. Levi seems enamored with you, or I should say, his stomach is. He says if you opened a diner, he'd never eat at home again."

More laughter filled April. "That is kind of him to say. Whatever the reason for you coming today, I am grateful. And, please, if there are any goods you want to sell here, there is plenty of space."

"Hmm," Naomi said. "My sisters and I do make quilts, but we usually consign them down at the diner where one of them works. But we make candles, too."

"*Wunderbar,*" April said as excitement at seeing her

dream become reality washed over her. "They'll be a hit with the *Englischers*, I'm sure."

Four hours later, after all the pies and jellies were sold, as well as some of Esther's quilts, April turned the sign to Closed and leaned against the locked door. She rested her hand on her belly and smiled at Esther. "We did it."

"No, my dear, you did it."

"Well, I certainly couldn't have done it without all your help making everything and cleaning the store." She couldn't have done it without Malachi either. Even though he had resisted the idea at first, he'd certainly helped her see her dream come to fruition. With him spreading the word, she'd had a lot of customers, *Englischers* and Amish alike, and she couldn't have been happier. Everything seemed to be going well. She had a place to live, a job, a business of her own, and a *boppli* on the way. All that was missing was confessing her feelings to the man who'd offered her marriage, but she couldn't do that, not without risking losing his friendship, her job and her business.

"I wish Malachi would have stuck around to see the success of the store," April said. "I need to thank him for all he's done to help me."

Esther hid a yawn behind her hand.

"Are you ready to go home?"

Esther nodded, and April turned down the lights. Together they walked across the alley and through the yard in the drizzling rain. "Soon, fall will be here, and the weather will grow colder."

"I know. I'm not looking forward to it. I suppose I'll need to make a few things for the *boppli* before it comes. All the clothing I had for Samatha burned in the fire."

"I think a shopping trip to the quilt shop is in order. They'll have what you'll want for the baby, and we won't have to hire a driver to go into the bigger town."

"I would like that," April said. She opened the screen door and held it for Esther when a scent rolled out from inside and caused her stomach to grumble. Somehow, she'd forgotten to eat lunch. She was surprised to find Malachi in the kitchen, cooking.

"Hello," he called out. "I thought after a long day, I should cook you something. Judging by the traffic, it looks to have been a *gut* day."

"*Jah*. I couldn't have asked for a better opening day," April said as she smiled at him. Sensing her eyes sparking with adoration for this man with a beautiful heart, she pushed the love she felt for him back into the shadows of grief and fear. She cleared her throat. "I believe I have you to thank for that."

One of his dark eyebrows arched. "What did I do?"

"You spread the word."

"Of course, you're part of this community, and that's what community does."

His words surprised her. The community she'd grown up in had been that way, but once she'd made the choice to leave, they'd locked the doors of affection and kindness to her. Making her feel as if her entire life had been nothing but a façade. David had kept her from forming connections within his community, even though many of the women had tried to pull her into their circle. During her road to recovery after his and Samantha's deaths, she'd once again felt like a burden.

"Levi helped, since I couldn't speak to how good your pies are. Can you believe I walked out without purchasing one?"

"That's okay," she said as she walked over to the counter and pulled back a linen towel from a pie plate. "I saved one for you."

With the table set, she and Esther washed up and sat at the table.

"It's not much, but it's what I know how to make," Malachi said as he placed a plate of grilled-cheese sandwiches in front of them along with a bowl of tomato soup. He opened the refrigerator and pulled out the salad April had made earlier in the morning and sat it in front of her. "And I thought, with the rain, and fall pressing against us, grilled cheese and tomato soup sounded good."

"*Denki*," she said. "I believe this is the most wonderful meal I've ever had." Only because it had been made from consideration for her. The thought sobered her. His gesture spoke more to the truth of what a real marriage should be. The union between a man and a woman was less about complete submission and more about being partners in life. Supporting each other in their day-to-day endeavors. Just like her parents had. Just as her *daed* did with his new wife. They worked together as a team, as one. Preferring each other over the other. Considering each other as worthy and valuable. She wanted that, and she wanted that with this man who made her feel as if she mattered.

"You haven't even tasted it," Malachi said, laughing as he pulled out his chair. "Shall we pray?"

They bowed their heads and prayed in silence. April thanked *Gotte* for the day, and for her life. She thanked Him for the loss and the grief, even though at the time of David and Samantha's deaths she hadn't been able to see a future on the other side of her emotional pain.

A soft cry rose from the bassinet and Malachi said, "Amen."

April shifted in her seat, ready to tend to Jeb's needs, but Malachi touched her arm as he rose from his chair. "Eat and relax."

She dipped her spoon into her soup and sipped the rich flavor into her mouth. "Mmm-mmm, this is *gut*."

"It is, Malachi. I taught you well," Esther snickered.

April watched Malachi as he changed Jeb then picked him up from the bassinet. "I'm glad you like it, especially now that you've tasted it."

Malachi pulled a bottle from a pan of warm water and sat back in his chair. Jeb's wide eyes focused on the plates and bowls on the table, but then he saw April and his smile brightened the room. He began kicking his feet as if he wanted April to hold him, and her heart warmed. She glanced at Esther, taking bites of her grilled-cheese sandwich, at Malachi wrestling Jeb in his arms, and she knew this was family. Her family. She only hoped Malachi would see her as family, too.

"I've decided to accept your offer," she said. "If it's still available."

Chapter Twelve

Jeb's baby bottle stilled in his hand, and it took him a moment to realize what April had referred to. "What changed your mind?"

"I've been thinking—"

"What offer is that?" Aunt Esther asked.

"Maybe we should speak after dinner," he said, noting that the rain seemed to have stopped as it no longer pattered on the metal overhang at the stairs.

By the time the table was cleared and the dishes done, Jeb had fallen back to sleep and Malachi had tucked him inside the bassinet. Aunt Esther, tired from the excitement of the day, snored in the rocker.

"I think we can speak in private now," April said.

Malachi scratched his jaw. "Let's go outside."

He donned his hat then held the door for April. He took one last look at Aunt Esther and Jeb before carefully easing the door shut so the creaking wouldn't stir his aunt and Jeb. They walked in silence toward the alley, April with her arms hanging at her sides. They reached the end of the gravel alley and April looked back at the house as they rounded the corner toward the front of the home-turned-businesses where he'd grown up.

"You had a good day?" he asked again, knowing they'd already talked about it. But he needed something to fill the space. His pulse had hammered from the moment she'd told him she had changed her mind, and he wasn't sure why. He wanted to marry her, but he wasn't sure his reasons had changed. Even in union, he'd have to keep his distance, and he'd insist she remain at Aunt Esther's while he and Jeb lived at his small house in the country. He couldn't afford to have his heart torn to pieces like his *mamm*'s had been when his father had chosen to leave her. He had to keep his emotions from being too caught up, for Jeb's sake.

"Oh, *jah*," she said. "It was better than I could have hoped for."

"As hard as you worked, you deserve success." He moistened his lips, and took in the warm, moist air caught between two seasons. "I'm proud of what you've done. It can't be easy to overcome the tragedy you've survived and press forward with such stubborn tenacity."

She looked up at him. "I'm not sure if you just complimented me or not, but *denki*."

"You knew what you wanted, and you went after it."

"I had little choice, if I was going to secure a future for myself and my *boppli*."

A car honked as it passed them on the road. One of his clients waved, and Malachi waved back.

"Some of your clients and their wives stopped by

today, all of them said great things about you. It is *gut* to know everyone sees the same man I do."

He tucked his thumbs into his suspenders as they turned another corner, the air much cooler in the shadow of the buildings. "Is that why you've changed your mind about my proposal?"

Her eyelashes fell against the curve of her cheek as she looked at the scarred hands resting on her swollen belly, full with his cousin's baby. "You were honest with me about the proposal, and I want to be honest with you." She paused in her footsteps and looked up at him. Her emerald-green eyes glittered. "I loved David, but I didn't when we married, and I'm not certain he ever loved me. He wanted a wife for convenience, to bear his sons, and care for his daily needs. He was rarely kind, and if I believe his comments, I was incompetent as a helpmate."

Malachi shook his head. "I hope you don't believe that."

"I don't, but I could have loved him more or loved him better. I suppose."

"Which is why my proposal was offensive to you?" Malachi asked, feeling his heart reach out to this small woman who was strong and courageous in her own right.

"It wasn't offensive, Malachi," she said. "I was afraid."

"And now?"

"I'm trying not to be. If I marry you, I want to continue with the store. It's important. David's death left me with nothing. I had no home, and no finances to support me. If I marry, I need to have the security that I can support myself."

"I understand," he said, knowing his mother had felt destitute whenever his *daed* disappeared for weeks at a time. He could only imagine how she'd felt when he'd left for good. The attached houses were hers, but only because they'd been left to her. If his grandfather hadn't given her property, she wouldn't have had anything but her sewing skills, and even then, she'd often felt she begged for work to feed her sons. "I wouldn't ask you to close your store, and if we come to an agreement, I will have a will written that both portions of the building remain with you."

"That is too much," she said.

Her humility tugged at his heart. "It's the least I can do for what you've done for us, and upon our marriage, what I know you'll do. Caring for Aunt Esther in her mental decline isn't easy, and I fear it will only become more difficult as time goes by."

"I have found that keeping her occupied helps, but with time, I worry that will no longer work."

"Before you agree, there is something you should know before you hear it from anyone else. My past is..." He paused, searching for the right words. "It's clouded in a lot of sin."

"You are the kindest and most considerate man I know. If you have a troubled past, it does not clothe you now."

"My father was a wastrel and chose the world over my *mamm* and Jared and I. He drank. A lot. I don't know if I ever saw him sober, and he was unfaithful. My *bruder* is like him, which is why I have Jeb."

She reached for his hand. "You are not your father's sins, or Jared's."

"It is nice of you to say so, but their actions have followed me everywhere. Speculation about whether I would follow their paths has always chased me."

"Then they don't know you, Malachi. You are not them, and it is obvious by the way you care for your family, your business, your clients and those who work for you, that your heart is pure and wholesome. I have known you a few weeks, a month now, and I can see your heart. You're a *gut* man."

"Would you ever worry I would become my father?"

She lifted her chin as if to defy an accusation. "No. That is the truth. I have fears David instilled in me, and I'm working on those. But I would never worry about you becoming a wastrel. You're a *gut* man, a *gut* Amish man."

His pulse pounded at her belief in him. He wanted to cry. Instead, he dragged in a shaky breath. "Then it's settled. We'll speak with Bishop Mueller about a wedding."

She shook her head. "Not yet. There is something you need to know."

He ran his thumbs along his suspenders and swallowed the tension knotted in his throat. "Go on."

"I realized earlier, after your proposal, that I love you."

His heart skipped several beats. He clenched his jaw. That was the last thing he'd expected her to say. "I—"

She held up her hand. "I don't expect you to feel the same, but since you were so honest with me about why you asked me to marry you, I wanted to give you the same courtesy and tell you why I have changed my mind. If you can marry a woman who loves you, then our arrangement is settled. If you can't, then we can try to go on as we have."

"April," he said, taking a few steps away from her and crossing his arms. Her confession made him want to accept her love, to reach out and hold it with his fists and never let it go. Even more, he wanted to love her. He did love her, but he couldn't. He wouldn't. For his sake, and for Jeb's sake. She'd spoken of her fears, but he hadn't spoken all his. In the years since his *mamm*'s death, he'd often found himself falling into thoughts that left him feeling as if the world was better without his presence. The very words his *mamm* had written in her note. Of course, he hadn't had those thoughts for many years, but the knowledge that he had had them at all plagued him, causing him fear that he would follow in his mother's footsteps if love failed him.

He raked his hand beneath his hat and tugged on his hair. "Love between two people is messy, and it's not something I believe in. Not for me, and not for you. I cannot love you, April." Yes, he loved Jeb and Aunt Esther, but they were safe to love. A woman who could destroy him and break his heart was different.

She nodded, even as tears sparked the corners of her eyes. "I understand."

"And I don't think I can marry you. Even though you say you don't expect my love, you will." Just as his mother had expected his *daed*'s. "You'll long for it day after day."

And he would never be able to confess the truth of his heart. He'd never be able to tell her he loved her. Not without fearing he'd succumb to his mother's illness.

"It's all right, Malachi," she said. "I've had my heart broken many times. It heals. I'll heal. And although I feared my confession could not be returned by you, I knew I couldn't marry you under false circumstances. I had to tell you the truth so you could make an informed decision."

"*Denki*," he said. "For your understanding."

He held out his hand to shake hers. "Then we'll continue as we've been. You'll care for Aunt Esther and Jeb and, of course, you'll keep your store. If ever any of it becomes too much, especially after your *boppli* arrives, then we'll adjust our agreement."

She reached out to shake his hand, but her nose twitched. She lifted her chin into the air and sniffed. Before he knew what was happening, she hiked her skirts and ran past him, toward Aunt Esther's home. He turned to follow her when he saw the smoke billowing out of one of the open windows.

Fear clenched his heart. "April!"

She kept running across the yard. He chased after her as he scanned the surrounding area.

Sirens pierced his ears. Fire trucks rolled to a stop in front of the house. It was then he saw a tearful Aunt Esther clinging to a lanky man holding Jeb, and it wasn't Mr. Gene, her neighbor. Malachi clinched his fists as he recognized his *bruder*. Had he caused the fire? Had he placed their aunt and Jeb in danger? The woman he loved?

He shifted his gaze toward the place he'd last seen April. She yanked the screen door open and vanished into the wall of dark smoke racing out of the house. He watched in horror as she disappeared inside.

"April!" He raced to the back steps and stretched out his arm for the door handle just as men dressed in their fire suits reached him and pulled him back. He tried to shake them off, kicking out his feet. "No! April! She's in there."

A man with heavy gear, a mask and a tank on his back darted inside.

"We'll find her," a firefighter said.

"You have to. Please, I didn't tell her I love her."

Gotte, no, not again, April screamed in her mind. She pressed her apron over her mouth and nose against the smoke assaulting her. It was difficult to see through the dark haze, but she focused on where Esther and Jeb had last been. Flames streaked up the blue curtains and licked at the feet of the bassinet. She raced across the room. The heat encompassed her, searing the scars on her hands. She hooked her leg around the bottom of the bassinet and pulled it closer to her, away from the red and orange heat devouring the house. She scrabbled around inside the bassinet and found it empty.

"Jeb! Esther!" she shouted through the apron and her hand as she darted madly through the downstairs, checking the pantry and other rooms. Finding it empty, she covered her hand with her dress and reached for the door leading upstairs. Memories assaulted her. A torrent of tears rushed down her cheeks, sticking ash and smoke to her flesh. She had to find them. She couldn't lose them like she'd lost David and Samantha.

April reached the landing, and with the air clearer, she dropped the apron from her face and searched the rooms. Esther and Jeb weren't in any of them. She turned toward the stairs and found dark smoke filling the hallway. She coughed, choking on the polluted air.

"What am I going to do?" She collapsed on the floor, holding her belly as if to hold her unborn baby in her arms. "I'm sorry. I'm so sorry."

Tears streamed down her face as she sucked in what little air she could. Her eyes closed and she couldn't find it in herself to open them. At least she'd told Malachi how she'd felt about him. That she loved him.

"I love you, Malachi and Jeb, and Esther," she choked. She silently thanked *Gotte* for allowing her to love such a wonderful man like Malachi.

Something pressed against her face and then a heavy blanket fell over her as complete darkness descended. She felt herself being lifted, but she couldn't figure out if it was real or memories from when she'd tried to rescue David and Samantha from their burning home.

She dug her fingers into the man's shoulder, expecting a thick fireman's coat. In her near unconscious state, she recognized a soft shirt. *Malachi?*

No, it couldn't be. The smoke infecting her lungs and stealing her oxygen were playing tricks on her mind. For a moment, she wondered if her confused state was anything like what Esther experienced each day.

"I've got you," a voice said near her ear. She tried

to attach it to Malachi's deep tones, but it wasn't him. "We're almost out."

The heavy blanket was pulled back and daylight smarted her eyelids. She tried to open her eyes to see who had rescued her, but the smoke still clung to the inside of her lids, causing them to burn. She squeezed them tight in an effort to ease the pain, but it didn't work. Unfamiliar sounds collided with familiar ones. As hard as she tried to distinguish them, she couldn't figure out what was in the here and now. The arms holding her released her to a soft mattress, and she pulled her eyes open. A fireman hovering above her placed a plastic mask over her face. She sucked in much-needed air, and then Malachi's handsome face appeared.

He drew his finger over her cheek. Was she dreaming? Had she died?

"April," he said. "You're too stubborn for your own good."

"Jeb," she croaked behind the oxygen mask. "Esther?"

"They are fine," he said. "I cannot believe you ran into a burning building."

"I c-couldn't lose them, too." She breathed in the fresh oxygen, and feeling better, she started to sit up. But Malachi guided her back down with his hand.

"I know, and I thank you for that."

"You saved me," she cried.

"No, Jared did," he said, and she couldn't help but recognize the relief in his voice. "He risked his own life to save yours, and it appears he saved Esther and Jeb, too. I guess he can't be all that bad."

"I love you," she said, not caring if he rejected her or denied her. "That's all I could think about."

"I love you, too," he said. "I knew that before, but thought it was better not to love you. I was too afraid of what loving you would cost me and Jeb. But when you rushed into the flames, I feared I'd lose you. I realized I was more scared of losing you to death than loving you. I promised I'd tell you what was in my heart. I promised I would be honest with you. I love you, April. I think I have from the moment you walked into my office."

"Then it's settled?" she said, hoping he understood what she was asking.

"*Jah*, it's settled, but we will talk after you're checked out at the hospital."

He bent down and pressed a kiss on her forehead, and she knew in that moment, with that small bit of affection, he'd told her the truth. Malachi Stoltzfus loved her.

Epilogue

Nervous energy raced through April's veins as it had the last five nights after their wedding.

She'd spent nearly a week in the hospital after the fire, and the only thing that had kept her from ripping out her IV and walking home was the assurance that Naomi and her sisters were keeping a close eye on Esther and Jeb since Malachi rarely left her side. Upon her discharge, she was surprised to find their community and the two other Amish communities in the area had come together and rebuilt Esther's home, but the layout was different and suited Esther's needs, which included three bedrooms on the bottom floor and two on the top so their great-aunt wouldn't have to navigate the stairs. The other rooms were for April, Malachi and the *bopplis*.

Moving into Esther's home had been an easy decision for them. Seems Levi had been looking for a place to buy where he could start a dog breeding business, and Malachi's home in the country was perfect for him. Of course, he'd care for the chickens until a barn and chicken coop could be built in the field across from Esther's house. Turns out the empty field belonged to

Malachi and Jared, inherited through their *mamm,* but Malachi, wanting to distance himself from memories wanted nothing to do with the property, until now, when new love healed old wounds.

Malachi explained the field would need to be cleared before they could plant crops, build a barn, and bring the chickens over, but he didn't want to do anything until he talked to Jared, who'd been squatting in the old barn hidden by decades of overgrown weeds and trees.

The even bigger surprise had been finding her father, Millie and all her *bruders* and *schwesters* had descended on Garnett to help with the rebuild and to keep her store running.

And knowing April and Malachi were to be married, they hadn't left. Surrounded by so much family, old and new, she felt blessed and well loved. Life couldn't be better.

April rolled onto her side and rubbed her hands against the tightening of her belly. It was good to see her family and to feel their hugs and love. And it seemed they wouldn't return home anytime soon since Millie declared they'd stay to help with the *bopplis.* April did not relish the day when her *daed* would pack up the *kinder* and Millie and leave. In her perfect world, she'd keep them close and continue building a relationship with her new *mamm.*

A sharp spasm rocked across her stomach, and she bit back the shock of it. She'd had some contractions over the last few days, but with all the busyness surrounding her, she'd pretended otherwise. Besides, she'd had a difficult time forgiving herself for leaving Esther and Jeb unattended while she and Malachi had gone out to speak about their future, and she wasn't quite sure she was ready to bring another life into the world. The responsibility was heavy and gut-wrenching.

Images of the smoke pouring out of Esther's house collided with the ones she recalled of the fire that had taken David and Samantha's lives. She'd never truly discovered what had caused the fire that killed David and Samantha, only that she'd awoken outside in the cold night to find her home engulfed in flames. She'd pressed into the heat, to save her child and husband, but it'd been too late.

She worried her bottom lip, thankful this time no lives had been lost. Still, she couldn't help thinking that if only she'd kept a better watch, the second fire wouldn't have happened. Malachi had tried to reassure her it was as much his doing as any, since he's the one who'd suggested they take a walk. Still, they both knew Esther's tendency to fade in and out of awareness in her mind. As it turned out, though, the fire had been nothing more than an accident when Esther knocked over a lantern as she'd stretched in her sleep in the rocker.

As Malachi had pointed out, besides April spending time in the hospital to make sure she and the baby were okay, all had worked out in the end. Esther had a new home where they could all live with their growing family. He'd even suggested the fire was a blessing, in that it was a turning point for his *bruder*. After all, seeing the smoke from his hiding place in the old barn, Jared had ushered Esther and Jeb to safety, and asked Mr. Gene to call the fire department. And then he'd entered a burning house to save the pregnant woman who'd showed him kindness when she'd had no obligation to do so.

Her husband seemed to marvel at the idea a man in as much trouble as Jared would stick around and not run the first chance he had, knowing law enforcement would arrive, too. Essentially, Jared had turned himself in for crimes he'd committed over the last few months. Her new *bruder* would spend some time in jail, but Malachi was hopeful he would return to the community and their faith. And somehow, Malachi thanked April for that blessing, when all she'd done was treat a stranger with compassion, as the Bible guided them to do.

She blinked into the darkness as another spasm rocked across her stomach. The *boppli* would make its appearance soon. In the next few days, maybe tonight, if the sharpening of each pain was any indication. She didn't want to alarm Malachi or Esther, so she rolled onto her back and stared at the ceiling, just as she'd done each night since her wedding night, waiting for Malachi's appearance.

They'd settled into a routine the last few nights since their wedding. He'd ask her if she was ready for bed, and taking it as a cue, she said yes. But then she'd lie in bed waiting, counting sheep, or running the fire through her mind, as silence held her until his footsteps fell softly down the hall and he slipped inside their room. He'd ease in beside her and intertwine his fingers with hers. Every morning, as she stirred to wakefulness, she basked in the feeling of his arm draped over her swollen belly. Not wanting to wake him, she'd remain motionless, curious about the sensation of being held by a man as tenderly as Malachi held her. This morning, he'd kissed her nape, and it had taken everything in her not to react because she didn't want them to be released from the love encompassing them. Tonight, she was determined to change the course of their routine. Tonight, she wanted to kiss him and hold him.

The knob turned on their door, and the soft glow of the lantern illuminated the ceiling.

"Hi," she said into the darkness.

Startled, he turned down the lantern. "What are you doing awake? Are you well?"

"*Jah*," she said. "I was just thinking."

He slid in beside her and, lying flat on his back with his hands folded over his chest, asked, "About the fire?"

"That," she said. "And us."

His breathing stilled, and she sensed his tension. "Should I be worried?"

"No," she said as she kissed his shoulder. "I'm so grateful for us."

"Me, too," he said.

She pushed up on her elbows and looked down at the man she called husband. The man who hadn't wanted a wife. The man she hadn't wanted to marry. "Esther did *gut* bringing us together."

He chuckled, and she saw the glitter of his eyes looking up at her. "That she did."

"Then why do you ignore me?"

"Ignore you? What are you talking about?"

She cleared her throat, unsure how to go about explaining her concerns. "You don't kiss me when you think I'm awake. You wait until you think I'm asleep before coming to bed and you leave before you think I'm awake. You don't—" The rest of her words were cut off by the sharp pain slicing across her stomach.

He sat up beside her and held her hand. "Are you okay?"

"Yes, I will be once you tell me why. Did you decide you don't love me?"

"Oh, *liebling*," he said, drawing her into his arms and sliding back down onto the mattress. "There is more to a relationship, more to a marriage, and more to intimacy than becoming physically one. And as much as I want to be a complete husband to you, we will wait until we are both ready. I fear once I kiss you, I will want more, and so, I ignore you, as you claim."

She thought about that for a moment as a tear rolled down her cheek. How had she been so blessed with a man to have so much consideration for her? *"Denki."*

"Of course," he said, and touched his mouth to her forehead. "Is there anything else?"

Her entire body tensed. She groaned then took several deep breaths until the contraction subsided. "*Jah*, will you go wake my stepmother? I believe we're about to have a baby."

After fixing the stairs, her father and the family had been staying in the rooms above the businesses so they could remain close to the store, and to her.

"Our baby is coming?" He released her and jumped out of bed then threw on his clothes. "Jeb is about to be a big *bruder*?"

She smiled into the dark, basking in the happiness overwhelming her and how accepting this man was of a baby not his own. She'd seen the way he treated Jeb as his own, and she knew he'd do the same with the baby she was about to have.

Malachi flung open the door.

"Malachi," she called before he left.

He turned toward her, knelt beside the bed, and took her hands in his. "Yes."

"I love you," she said.

He pressed his mouth to her lips for several long seconds. This was their first kiss since they'd said their vows and she drank him in, hungering for more. His beard felt nice against the softness of her cheek. This man, this husband of hers, was a *wunderbar* man, and she'd thank Gotte for him every day for the rest of her life. Her body clenched into the spasm and he pulled back as he jumped to his feet. "I love you, too, April. We're having a baby!"

With that, he raced out the door. April didn't think she'd ever been happier in her life, and then a few hours later, watching the man she loved hold their little girl in his arms as tears streamed down his face, she knew it to be true.

* * * * *

Dear Reader,

Thank you for, once again, spending time in Garnett, Kansas. Amish don't typically live in town, but in an effort to touch on a topic many of us are aware of and have experienced, I wanted a neighbor to expose Great-Aunt Esther's dementia to Malachi, who is determined to avoid his aunt's declining health. Therefore, I took creative license to bring to light the challenges of caring for our aging loved ones and wrote Esther living on the edge of town. Even though April has no experience with dementia, she makes the perfect caregiver because her heart seeks to understand people, especially Esther's needs and allows her some freedom—freedom April, herself, longed for when confined to a life less than optimal.

I hope you enjoy April and Malachi's story. As always, you can contact me at authorchristinarich.com.

Thanks,
Christina